A story that's based on murder, domestic violence,
and incarceration  could only
be titled.....

# HOOD
# STRUGGLE

## -TRILOGY-

For information about special discounts for bulk purchases, please e-mail Kevinguillard@yahoo.com
kevinguillard@facebook.com

The book that you are about to read is based on a true story, but everything about it, isn't real. Some of the characters as well as some of the events where added from the imagination and told strictly to enforce the objective. The characters that were added was Lil' Troy, Carl, Joe, Lil' Tim, and Jon-Jon. Although, Lester is actually a person, all of the events that took place with him in "Hood Struggle", isn't real. Every character name, but some of those that are no longer with us, was substituted. All of the lives in "Hood Struggle", other than the 5 that I just told you, are real and were either rounes or associates of mines.

The purpose of me writing this book was to see if I could open a few eyes in the urban neighborhoods. We're seeing it happen every time we turn our television to the 5:00 news channel or when we simply open the front doors and take a step outside. It's happening so close that it's now under the same roof as us. I think that I'll be fair and accurate to say that out of 95% of the families in the urban neighborhoods, there's at least one member that's been incarcerated before, whether it's a brother, sister, uncle, or a parent. Some families have relatives that are never coming home again, and to those my heart goes out. To the families that have lost a love one by the hands of a gun, my deepest sympathies and my heart goes out.

My name is, Kevin Antoine Guillard, I'm 25 years old and currently incarcerated. I haven't been here for that long this time; only about 2 years and 5 months. The other night when I called out there, I was told that my lil' cousin, Dan Smith, was murdered coming from one of the clubs in Baton Rouge. On my last jose, I lost a grandmother and too many of my rounes. It's always hard whenever you lose a love one regardless of where you may be at the time it happened, but damn it's hitting me extra harder in here. Dan was only 22 years old so he had his whole life ahead of him. I already shed my tears, punched the walls and kicked on the iron toilet in my cell, so I guess I'm feeling a lil' better now. That still doesn't take away from what it is, and that's, fucked up!

Being that I'm locked up in the feds, I wasn't allowed to attend his funeral. Whenever you're in a federal prison, no matter who dies in your family, you can't go see them. They leave you with no choice but to stay in your cell and do whatever you gotta do to get over it without adding any more time to your sentence, if you're short to home. I don't have that much time left myself. Matter of fact, about time you get this, I'll already be at the crib, this time for good. I let the prison system take all the fight out of me. After this jose, I'm not trying to give these people one more day out of my life. I'ma keep it 100, I miss my momma.


CEASE THE VIOLENCE/INCREASE THE PEACE
Enjoy the Read

Proverbs 14:12
There's a way that appears to be right,
but in the end it leads to death

In Memory Of

Hattie May Guillard, Dan Smith, and Henreatte "Tinibit" Guillard

-Also-

16th Lil' Danger, 16th Tavoris, 16th Jersey Phat, B.L. Ced,

13th Lil' Bleek, 17th PJ's Tonya, 16th Tricky, 16th Dirty Red, 17th

Future, Convention St. Ceasure, Convention St. Lil' D, Convention St.

Buck-Buck, Myrtle St. Bobby, 12th Bush Wick, B.L. Muscle Head,

and for all of the falling soldiers from my hood to ya hood

**Comments:**

Demetris White                              RN Baton Rouge General Hospital

October 20, 2013

Hi, I'm reading your book now it was bought for me as a gift, and I must say I'm truly enjoying it. Keep up the good work, looking forward to reading many more.




Dawn Dirisu                                 Mother of Sara

September 8, 2015

I just got finished reading the book. So good so good! I want to read the next one now..! But I'm gonna wait. I know it's going to be so good! Thank you for the opportunity to see inside of your imagination! One of many of your biggest fans, Dawn.

# "1998"

(Antoine)

Damn Monique talking loud... Is that Crystal and Tonya I hear in there too...

Aw man, it must be about 12:30 or 1:00 and I'm still here, sleeping. I don't need Monique tripping on me today. She's already lettin' me stay here. Even though I know that's just until I mess up too many times where she'll have a good enough reason to put me out. Well, I guess I can add today to another one of those mess ups. What I need to do is take that garbage bag off the window; it's pitched dark in here. She's been waking up before me ever since I decided to block out the sun light. Man let me get up, hit my grill and get dressed, so I can get out this woman's apartment.

"Monique, you should've come with us to Chatter Box last night," Crystal said, "You not gon' believe what the wind blew in."

"Girl who y'all saw," Monique asked.

"Girrrl, while me and Tonya was sitting at the table with Kevin and two of his boys, guess who we see walking through the doe looking like new money?" Crystal continued without waiting for an answer. "That fine ass baby daddy of yours."

"Girl, fuck Lester!" Monique expressed.

"No bitch, your other baby daddy." Crystal replied.

"Girl, stop lying," Monique said, putting her full attention back on Crystal.

"She not lying girl," Tonya agreed. "I saw Jon-Jon with my own eyes."

"Oh, I wonder when he got out." Monique openly asked herself.

"I can't tell you when he got out, but I can tell you that he was looking like he never went to jail to begin with," Crystal exclaimed. "I'm talking 'bout two herringbones wrapped around his neck. Not one but two. Plus, he was polo down; fresh from head to toe."

"Was he by his self?" Monique asked.

"I think he came there with the Shepherds," Crystal answer. "Well that's who he left with."

"That boy still haven't learned," Monique said. "You would think after doing a year in the parish behind Carl Shepherd that he would get the picture and stay away from them."

"Fa'real girl, how do you get so high that you drop your dope in someone else's car," Tonya asked.

"That's that other stuff Carl and the rest of them Shepherds be messing with. I wouldn't be surprised if Jon-Jon became a member of their sniffing session also. Birds of a feather," Crystal stated.

Monique shakes her head indicating her disapproval of the matter. "I can't believe how that boy is messing up his life. Jon-Jon got so much of potentials but he always let his self get involved around the wrong crowd. I really hope he wakes up and realize that the Shepherds don't mean him any good before it's too late."

"Monique, girl you're talking like you still in love," Crystal said. "Bitch you must've forgotten that you're three months pregnant and currently playing wifey to Lester."

"Well damn bitch, Jon-Jon was my first love and even though his cheating ass couldn't keep his dick in his pants, he still is J.J and Jonathan's daddy. With that being said, yea I love him and always will. We just could never be in a relationship again. He's too caught up in them streets. Now as for Lester, I'ma beat him up whenever he come walk through that door."

"Oh Lawd, what Lester do this time?" Tonya asked.

"Don't know how to come home at night." Monique answered. "It's 3:00 in the afternoon and he haven't called or anything. I wonder what lame excuse he'll try to come with this time cause he starting to make this a habit."

"I think your nephew just got up," Tonya said.

"Yea I hear him in the bathroom," Monique replied.

"Tonya he must've partied harder than we did; wakin' up at this time." Crystal said.

"He was prolly just over at Big Mike's house with Blue

Black." Tonya said, in my defense.

"Girl now he started hanging with Andy around that Greyhound Bus Station, and I think he's selling dummies too." Monique said.

"What makes you say that?" Tonya asked.

"Because the other day I went washed them kids' clothes out, and when I came back and put'em in the room, I looked on the bed where Antoine sleep and found a plastic bag with three lil' pieces of rocks in it."

"Girl stop lying!" Tonya said.

"I'm serious," Monique told her. "So I went and showed the stuff to Lester and that's when he told me it's not real."

"Have you talked to Antoine yet?" Crystal asked.

"Not yet, but I'ma talk to him though," Monique answered, while hearing the bathroom door open.


"What's up Monique," I asked my auntie, as I came in the living room.

"Nothin', Antoine what time did you come inside last night," Monique asked.

"It wouldn't too late," I answered. "I think at about 12 or 12:30."

"Antoine we need to talk so try not to be gone too long," Monique said.

~ 6 ~

"Alright, I ain't gon' be long."

"Blue Black came by here lookin' for you," Monique told me.

"How long ago that's been?" I asked.

"About an hour," Monique answered.

"Alright Monique," I said, while walking toward the front door.

"Alright," She replied.

**As soon as I step foot outside**, I'm greeted by the daily aroma of Big D's project hallways. A smell that for the first 6 months of me being over here, it forced me to cover my nose with the top of my shirt and hold my breath to keep from throwing up. Now don't get it bent, I'm 100 percent hood. It's just that this is my first time ever living in the projects. Living here with my auntie Monique, I'm being introduced to a lot of firsts. Like what happen last night. That was my first time ever staying out in the streets until nearly 4:00 in the morning. My momma wasn't having it. Not to mention her husband, Pastor Frankling.

By me saying my momma husband's name, you should already understand my reasons of coming to live with my auntie. To those that's from the other side and not the gutta side, a street person can't be living with a pastor. It's too many rules. Besides that, it's a few other reasons that led to me being here. Before we get into all that though, let me tell you a few things about the pastor.

He drives 18 wheelers for a living so he's gone most of the time which is a good thing. My momma has been married to him now for about 4 years, since I was nine. And for the most part, the pastor is cool. He buys my momma just about anything she wants; expensive clothes and nice cars. Plus, he gives me and my older brother allowances after almost ever run he makes.

By the way, I have 1 older brother name Trap that's 15 years old. My lil' brother Jamine is 8 and my lil' sister Lashay is 7. Everyone call me by my middle name which is Toine, short for Antoine, and I'm 13 years old.

Like I was saying, the pastor is cool but there's this one problem that spells destruction in big bold letters; his bad habit of talking with his hands. I'm a man myself so I can't be lettin' another man put his hands on me. Plus, I think he put his hands on my momma before, but I'm not 100 percent positive.

There was this one time when my momma was washing a glass out in the kitchen sink and I just so happen to walk pass her to get a cold drink from out of the refrigerator. Before I opened the refrigerator door, I glanced at my momma and noticed a mark on her face. Being that we had to deal with a few abusive men in the past trying to put their hands on her, by me seeing that mark I automatically jumped to the conclusion. When I asked her about it she told me that she scratched herself while she was doing her hair. The way that she said it sounded convincing enough to make me drop it, but not enough to make me believe her.

When an incident occurred maybe a month later where she ended up falling and breaking her arm, well she said she fell, but it was only the two of them in the room at the time. After we all returned from the hospital, the pastor ended up leaving the house. While he was away, my momma found Trap in the bathroom loading one of the pastor's rifles. I guess that's when she realized how serious we were.

As a result, the next time the pastor went on the road my momma had us to pack up all of our clothes because she was leaving him. She was still denying that he had ever put his hands on her, but she was leaving him because she said "we" thought he did. We moved to Conroe, Texas to a friend house that she met through him. You probably have a good idea to how this turned out. We stayed in Texas for nearly a month and we even transferred schools to the public schools in the district of where their mutual friend, Mrs. Dills lived.

Trap was in the 10th grade so he went to Peet High. Jamain and Lashay both were in the second so my momma enrolled them in Lanier Elementary. I was in the eighth grade over at Peet Junior High. The school that I went to was ok in my opinion. The only problem was that they had too many white folks for me. I think I was like one out of five blacks in the whole school and then those blacks don't really classify as being black in my book. Needless to say, I stayed solo.

I didn't have to put up with the problem for too long though. Before we could even get situated, the pastor came out to Ms. Dills' house and convinced my momma to come back to Baton Rouge, Louisiana/back to him.

The last time he put his hands on me was exactly what I just said; the last time he'll put his hands on me. I had gotten into some trouble at school and was put on punishment so I couldn't leave the house. Well while I was punished, the pastor had to go on the road and needed my momma to go with him so she could help him drive. Before they left the house though, the pastor decided to call his deacon over and told him to stay at the house until they came back in town. No disrespect to the church, but that sounded a lot like a watch dog to me. Anyway, I jumped on my lil' brother bike and went to the south by this lil' brod house by the name of Baby T.

When my momma and the pastor came back, the pastor started yelling at me and ended up punching me in the chest. Time for a little clarification: The pastor is not my biological father. My real dad left us when I was four years old and haven't been back since so I'm not about to let another man just come into the picture and start putting his hands on me. Understand that I'm far from scary, it just that the pastor is far from small or anywhere near my size. He's about 6'5, big, and loves to brag about him being a black belt. One time he even wore his karate suite to the church and tried to give the congregation karate lessons. Imagine that, men and women as big as 290 pounds kicking and chopping. Moving out was the only reasonable thing that I could think of.

After packing my bags, I gave Jamain the number to Monique's house and told him that if he ever heard any kind of noise coming from momma's room, like them arguing or anything, to call me A.SAP. Trap was still living there so I wasn't worried too much, but there was always that, "what if…"

Coming to the south, which is my original stomping grounds, was the best decision I could've made. Monique goes to the club a lot so the only thing that she ever ask me to do is watch her two boys for her when she's out and to take out the trash whenever I see it's full. Her son J.J is 5 and her other lil boy Jonathan is 4 so it's not like I'm baby sitting and have to put up with the crying, bottles, and diapers. Watching them is no problem. She usually goes out on Friday, Saturday, and sometimes on Wednesday, but since she got pregnant she slacked up a lot. I still try to make sho' I be around on those days.

I've been living here for a little bit over two months now and in my opinion everything's been going good. Other than me being around to watch her kids I try to stay away. I figured the less she sees me the less chances I have of becoming a problem. Damn, I can't believe I stayed asleep all this time. Usually I come in when she's in the bed and I'm out before she wakes up.

That, "Antoine we need to talk," didn't sound too good. She shouldn't tell me that I have to leave, because I'm hardly there anyway. On top of that, I stopped eating from her house a long time ago, compliments of my dog Andy teaching me how to hustle in different ways.

Before Andy's doctrine, jacking was my MO. One night when I first came over here, I found a .25 in one of the cuts by the Greyhound Bus Station. It's broke, plus I don't have a clip for it, but at night time the last thing on those junkies minds is, "How is he gonna shoot the gun with all that tape wrapped around it?"

All they're worried about is this aggressive young man that has a blue bandana wrapped around the lower part of his face, screaming at'em, "Come up out them pockets!"

Since Andy put me on the hustle, I don't have to take the

stick'em up route no more. The dummy game makes it to where I can rob'em with a smile on my face. Although, sometimes they try to get smart and ask me to let them taste it first before they buy it. When that happens, oh well, back to faze one. "Come up out them pockets you crack head!"


Today was like any other day in South Baton Rouge; sun blazing, lil' kids running around playing, and more heat. Today it felt like at least 110 degrees with no kind of breeze. I spot my dog Blue Black sitting on the bench in the projects' park with a towel wrapped around his head.

"What's up roune?" I asked Blue Black, as I walked up to him and dapped him down. I sat on top of the bench on side of him. Blue Black is crayon black, short, kind of stalky from him doing some time in L.T.I juvenile correctional facility, and has four gold teeth at the top of his mouth. I haven't known Blue Black for that long. I remember seeing him throughout the south a couple years back, but we've only been kicking it since I've been living here in the projects. Him and my dog Andy were cousin so the three of us ran together hard.

"Cooling," Blue Black answered. "I just left from over there looking for you. Monique said you were still sleep.

"Yea she told me."

"At first I thought you were gone with Andy. Big Mike told me that he seen Andy passing early this morning in a rental." Blue Black said.

"Who car Andy in," I asked.

"He in Rock car," Blue Black answered.

"Who," I asked again; not remembering who the hell is Rock.

"You know, that black Saturn Lil' P always in." Lil' P was off of Brice Street. He was around the same age as me and Blue Black and considered as one of the big dogs throughout the top; real nigga fa'real. When Blue Black told me the Saturn Lil' P always in, I knew exactly what car he was talking about. "I've been sitting here for over an hour now and that nigga ain't passed through here yet."

"Have you checked by Seni's house?" I asked.

Blue Black took a second to guzzle down the last from the 7up bottle he was drinking. "As soon as Big Mike told me about it that was the first place I checked. She said she hasn't seen him since yesterday evening. Ain't no telling how long Andy had the rental.

"Both of us were together at the bus station last night," I said.

"What time was that?" Blue Black asked.

"I busted out at 'round 3:30."

"Let's go chill by Big Mike's house," Blue Black said. We both got up and started walking.

Big Mike's house is where almost everybody from 17th street be chilling at. It's always something going on; card games, dominos, or just sitting around drinking and getting high. Big Mike was around 28 or 29 years old and placed on official O.G.

status. He must've had his whole family staying with him. I think it was like twelve or thirteen people living in that four bedroom house. He got this one cousin living there name Iesha that be checking me out on the cool. She thinks that I don't be paying attention. I'ma see what's up though.

Big Mike's house was right on the side of the projects. After we took the 20 second walk that it took to get there, Blue Black sat in the recliner chair that they kept on the porch. By us sitting on the porch, we'll still be able to see when Andy passes through. I grabbed one of the crates from off the side of the steps and brought it on the porch. I sat on the crate and watched Blue Black reach down and pulled out a nickel bag of weed from his left sock along with a keep moving cigar that was sticking out.

"Did you and Andy come up on somethin' last night?" Blue Black asked, as he used the finger nail from his thumb to cut open the cigar.

"Yea, we came up on a lil' somethin'. It took damn near all night, but when the bus from Houston came in and three megos jumped off it, we knew our luck was about to change. Andy approached them, and sho' as shit stank, he served them. I watched it from across the street. The three megos walked between the two buildings in the back of the bus station and that's when Andy came over and asked me how many dummies I had."

I grabbed the blunt from Blue Black and hit it a few times before I continued. "I told him I had four dubs and three dimes, so he told me to give it to him 'cause they only asked for a dub. That's when Andy looked at me like, 'how in the world do three Mexicans get high off of one dub?' Good thing Andy had some real dope on him.

We watch the three megos come back from visiting with Scotty. When they saw Andy, they called him over and asked him to give them something for 200."

Blue Black busted out laughing. "They fell for the okey doke."

"Every time," I said. "After that, me and Andy walked to Convention Street and split the money. He said that he had six dummy dimes that he put with the ones I gave him and he gave all of it to the megos. He also said that it was a good thing they only asked him for a dub at first, 'cause that was all the real dope he had left. If they would've asked him for a thirty then he would have served them three dummy dimes and messed up that $220 lic'.

We chilled on Convention and waited for the Houston bus to leave then Andy went back to continue talking to the lil' brod that worked there. I busted out. I didn't have any more dummies on me so there was no reason for me to go back."

"Mane bruh, somethin' told me to come over there last night," Blue Black complained.

"Blue Black that was the only thing that happened then that took forever."

"Something else prolly came when you left, and that's prolly when Rock came through with the rental." Blue Black said.

"Where you was anyway?" I asked. "Andy kept asking if I saw you."

"I was messing around by Tracy's house," Blue Black answered.

"So you finally hit?"

Blue Black dropped his chin into his chest and started shaking his head from left to right. "Mane I still ain't hit. When we got in her bedroom, she went in her closet and pulled out a bottle of Hennessy. She got to talking so much that before I knew it I was drunk. Mane bruh, I passed out right in her bed."

"Where her momma was?" I asked.

"Her momma work's overnight now," Blue Black answered. "She just got a job at Circle K on Highland road, but 'bout time we woke up her momma was already coming through the front doe, so Tracy tells me to jump out the window. I looked at her like she just got finished smoking one of them hard pieces. I told her if she would've given me some last night then I prolly would. I got up and walked straight out the front doe."

"I knew I heard Blue Black out chea!" Spider said, as he came outside scratching his bald fade wearing head. Spider is one of Big Mike's younger brothers; dark skinned, tall, skinny, and funny looking. He's the comedian of the family; cooler than a fan. "Y'all getting high on my porch and don't knock on the doe to tell me nothin'. Boy that's cold bloody."

"Come on Spider, I never seen a village get high off of one blunt." Blue Black said, then took a big hit off of it.

"Mane, forget all that. Pass the blunt Blue Black! You over here trying to kill it before it get to me." Spider said, while walking over to Blue Black to get the roach from him.

15 minutes after Spider came out, everybody else from inside the house started coming out. We bullshitted around for prolly 'bout 30 minutes then Big Mike pulled into the parking lot with two ounces of killa. I walked over to him and told'em to take me up the street to the store Romano's so I could get a couple cases of beer.

When we made it back from the store, everybody was standing around in the parking lot. Big Mike pulled in and grabbed the two cases from the back seat. I grabbed the two bags of ice. Big Mike sat the beers on the ground then called out to Spider and told him to get the ice cooler from out the backyard.

Spider rinsed out the cooler with the hose pipe then brought it over and filled it up with the ice and beers. I watched Big Mike reach inside of his car through the rolled down window of his old school grey Monte Carlo and put his car key in the ignition. Moments later, we heard Cash Money's B.G blaring from Big Mike's 6x9's.

"On dangerous grounds, with the k up in my hand

ready to bust that ass. Mr. Clean Up Man.

On dangerous grounds, with the k up in my hand

ready to blucka blast. Mr. Clean Up Man."

We all stood around drinking and tripping off of Spider's crazy ass as the time rolled by. Then out the blue, well you could say out the dark, guess what night creature comes crawling from around the corner? Yep, Mr. Move Maker Andy, with a 40 ounce bottle of Old English in his hand. He went over and gave Big Mike some dap then came and dapped down me and Blue Black.

"Andy nigga where you been," Blue Black asked.

"Messing 'round in the bottom," Andy answered.

"What the hell you doing in the bottom," Blue Black said, with his face frowned up.

"I was down there by Nikki's house." Andy answered.

"Nigga you been by a bitch house all this time?"

"I meant to come back and pick you up Seni, but I was in the middle of something." Andy said.

Blue Black stopped talking for a minute and thought about who Andy had called him, then about the way he was acting. Everybody bust out laughing. "Damn, I must be drunk," Blue Black
admitted to his self.

"Andy, you gave the whip back," Big Mike asked.

"Not yet," Andy answered. "I got it parked around the corner."

"Andy boy I seen you passing early this morning looking like you was on a mission." Big Mike told him.

"I wouldn't on one then, but I was damn sho' trying to find one." Andy replied.


Andy threw the Old English bottle in the grass across the

street and grabbed a cold beer from the cooler. As he walked back toward me and Blue Black, he signaled with his eyes for us to follow him.

We started walking in the direction of the bus station. Andy asked did any one of us have any dummies. Blue Black shook his head, no, and I told him, "'Bout time I woke up it was 3:00 so I wouldn't able to make anymore because Monique was already up."

Andy told us that he needed to make some more money, because he used $60.00 to score a 16th from Big Thug and he gave two dubs of that to Rock for the rental.

"When you suppose to take it back to him," Blue Black asked.

"I gave him the two dubs for nine hours, but later on tonight I'ma go take him another lil' thirty or something." Andy replied.

"You should of just gave him some dummies," Naive me.

"Toine, boy you trying to get Andy killed," Blue Black said, through laughs. "If Andy would've gave Rock some fake rocks, he would've found Rock waiting on him in the bushes with that rusty .38 he be having."

Andy told us that he might have some dummies hidden by the bus station. He did. We stayed there for 30 minutes to an hour before Andy lucked up and caught a $40.00 sell, which was well worth it.

On our way to get the car, we passed by the Shepherds

house and three of them were standing outside. Me and Andy followed Blue Black as he started walking towards them. The closer we got, the better I began to make out their faces. I noticed it was Brian Shepherd, Lil' Wick Shepherd, and Jazz Shepherd. I didn't really know Brian or Lil' Wick Shepherd, but I had heard about them throughout the hood. Plus, they both had the kind of cars that made it so where everybody knew who they were.

Brian had an Old School money green Cadillac with peanut butter insides sitting on some 20" Dayton's. Lil Wick had a burgundy Cadillac with flacks in the paint job and that "main line" in the trunk. His music was so loud that you could hear it from three blocks away. He had his sitting on 20" D's too. I knew Jazz Shepherd from school. We were both in the 6th grade together at South East Middle.

While Andy and Blue Black went dapped down Brian and Lil' Wick Shepherd, I went and gave Jazz some dap.

"Detention Blue Black, what's good roune?" Brian Shepherd asked Blue Black, during the daps.

"We cooling," Blue Black answered. "What's going down wit' y'all boys tonight?"

Lil Wick hand Blue Black the blunt he was smoking on. "Come on nah Blue Black, you should already know what's up with us. Saturday night Vibe's, babyyyyy!"

"Damn, we forgot all about Vibes tonight," Blue Black said, while looking at Andy. "Andy, you know Vibe's be hoe city on Saturday nights."

"We gon' fall in that bitch tonight," Andy assured Blue Black.

"Andy, who car y'all in," Brian Shepherd asked.

"I got Rock car parked around the corner." Andy answered.

"Vibe that thang then, niggaaaa," Lil' Wick over expressing everything he said.

"We gon' fall in. What time you boys heading that way?" Andy asked Brian Shepherd.

"We 'bout to leave in about 15 or 20 minutes," Brian replied. "Go get the whip and y'all could follow behind us."

"Cool," Andy said. Me and Andy then turned around and started walking down the street, leaving Blue Black behind.

On our way, we passed back by Big Mike's house and seen that everyone was still standing outside. Still smoking and drinking with the music on full blast. Andy told me that he had to holla at Big Mike right quick.

While Andy was walking off, I looked to my right and saw Big Mike's lil' sister, Pat, walking toward me with a smile on her face. I turned to face her. She grabbed my arm as we began walking. She asked if I knew that her cousin Iesha was digging me. I told her no then I asked where Iesha was. Pat started smiling again then asked if I wanted to holla at her. I told her yea and to tell her cousin to come talk to me. More smiles as she told me to hold up a second and walked off.

Moments later, Iesha came walking toward me wearing a

pair grey shorts that revealed a camel toe that had to be the size of my fist. Along with the matching grey top that showed off her flat belly with the perfect belly piercing. A nice size C-cups that looked so soft that they were like magnets to my eyes, and even though she was wearing a sports bra, her nipples was trying to burst through the fabric. As she walked closer to me, I had to literally strain my eyes to move away from them.

"Hey Antoine," Iesha said, standing not even a foot away from me. I had to look down at her 'cause Iesha was only about 5' even, if that. Just the way I like it.

"What's going down wit'cha?" I asked.

"You," Iesha stated, point blank and simple. A female that gets straight to the point is never a bad thing with me.

"That's what's up," I said. I noticed Andy walking toward me out the corner of my eyes. "You finna go somewhere Antoine?" Iesha asked.

"Yea," I answered. "But if I could, I'ma try to come back over here tonight."

Iesha grabbed my hand and put a piece of paper in it. As she walked off, I saw that she had a smiley face on the back of her shorts. I made a mental note to get back at her, A.SAP.

When me and Andy reached the car and got inside, he hand me a nice size bag of weed along with three cigars. I went in my pocket and pulled out a $10.00 bill. I put the money in an empty space that was under the tape deck and told him, "You could use that later on for some gas or something."

"That's what's up," Andy replied.

As soon as we got to the Shepherd's house, we saw Blue Black and Brian getting in Brian's lac while Lil' Wick and Jazz jumped in the other lac. We followed suite.

I met Andy and Blue Black at the same time by Big Mike's house. When me and Andy started talking to each other, just like that, we clicked and have been running together on a daily basis since. Monique don't like me hanging around Andy 'cause she think that our age is too far apart for us to have anything in common. Andy is 19, about 6.2, light brown with two gold teeth on the side.

On our way to the club, I asked Andy if they checked for I.D's.

"I never seen them ask anyone for an I.D," Andy told me. "Look at Blue Black. He's only 15 years old and he stay in Vibe's, and your lil' roune Jazz Shepherd around that same age."

When we crossed the Mississippi Bridge to Port Allen, where Club Vibe's was located, we got jammed in from all the cars going in the same direction. Andy told me that's one of the reasons he hated coming to Vibe's; 'cause all of the traffic. "This one of the easiest ways to get at somebody; stuck in traffic on a two-way street. All you have to do is be coming from the club with some tinted windows on your car and see your enemy sitting next to you. While he's smoking on some good green and bobbing his head up and down you loading up a hundred rounds in the chopper, smiling at him. Park your car at the Waffle house we just passed, get out, run back, and unload on him and

~ 23 ~

whoever else he in the car wit'."

After sitting in traffic for at least 45 minutes, we finally pulled into the club's parking lot. We parked the cars, got out, and made our way to club's entrance. At the time, I'm thinking that we must have been in a rush because we were passing up everybody standing in the line. We got to the front door and Brian Shepherd exchanged a few words with a big black dude that had brads in his head. A short while later, the dude removed a rope to let us pass. Blue Black, Jazz, Lil' Wick, and Brian went through, but when my time came, the panther looking mutha fucka holds out his arm and shakes his head, "No".

Me and Andy had already started cussing the bitch out when Brian Shepherd came and said that I was wit' him. Brian Shepherd must have been a regular at the club because the dude told Brian, "Alright, but make sho' you watch him in there." After Brian Shepherd said he got me, the oil spill let me pass.

As soon as we got inside, I saw people standing around everywhere. I tried to make my way through the crowd in the same direction that Brian Shepherd was going in, but I couldn't see anything. Somebody kept flashing the lights on and off. While I was going through my state of confusion and not believing that the inside of a club actually looked like this, I felt somebody's arm wrap around my neck and pull me towards him. Next thing I know is that person yelling in my ear and telling me to stay close to him. That's when I realized it was Andy.

We finally got through the crowd to a section where it seemed like the whole South Side Uptown was posted up at. I saw Brian Shepherd go over and dap down a gang of niggas then he grabbed a bottle of Hennessy from one of'em. Andy dapped down a few people also then we turn to face the same way as the rest of the south. Andy reached in his pocket and pulled out one of the blunts I rolled up in the car.

While Andy sparked up, I looked at the niggas that I was standing with to see how many faces I noticed. Most of them were people that I've been seeing on a day to day basis since living with Monique. As I looked a little deeper, I saw J.J and Jonathan's daddy, Jon-Jon, getting the bottle of Hennessy from Brian Shepherd.

The first thing that came to my mind was, "I thought that he was locked up." Then I wondered if Monique knew he was out..... Monique.... Damn, she usually goes out on Saturday nights; I forgot all about her. And didn't earlier she say that she wanted to talk to me about something? Mane fuck! I'm fuckin' up. As I was caught up in my thoughts of hoping Monique didn't wanna go out tonight, I felt Andy nudge me on the arm to give me the blunt.

I hit it a couple of times then looked over by the dance floor and saw the biggest ass I ever seen in my life. She was about 5.2, caramel complexion, with an ass that was complimented by the prettiest set of thighs I ever seen also. I'm not sure if it was her ass being big or those pink shorts she was wearing being small. All I saw was ass checks hanging out.

Lil' Wick Shepherd must have seen me in a zone, probably wit' my tongue hanging out, because he came over and started pulling me by the arm toward her direction. When he got close enough to where he could reach out and grab her, he grabbed her arm and pulled her a step or two back. We were pressed right up against each other.

She turned around to see who I was. Next thing I knew is that she started throwing that ass, left, right, up, down, back, back, and back. That ass was moving so fast on me that I didn't know what to do. I looked over at Lil' Wick Shepherd, who was standing a few feet away from us.

"Do ya thang nigga. Do ya thang," Lil Wick yelled, while nodding his head up and down and showing his four gold teeth across the top. Lil Wick looks just like Spider, except Spider don't have any gold in his mouth.

While the girl bent over and put both of her hands on her knees, I grabbed her by the waist and started shaking on that ass. I shook on her for prolly about four songs straight. I thought I was really doing something. That is until the club closed and everybody busted out.

As soon as me, Andy, and Blue Black got in the car and closed the door, the two of them busted out laughing like they was watching the movie Friday for the first time. Talking about I looked like a robot going out of service. I wouldn't trippin though. All I know is that I got to feel on the biggest ass in the club, and I ain't see them dancing wit' nobody, so take that.

The club closed at 2:00. Andy told us that he was surprised nobody got shot. Vibe's usually ended in gun smoke. Blue Black told us about the time when he went there a couple weeks back and a nigga opened fire on the middle of the dance floor.

After we crossed the bridge, back to East Baton Rouge, Andy told us that he met a brod at the club that wanted him to call her as soon as he left. Blue Black asked if she had a sister or a friend. Andy told him that he didn't know, but he think he saw her wit' some more brods so he was gonna check and see. I told Andy that he could drop me off. I was really feeling the effect of the weed that we had been smoking on all night. He asked me if I was sho' because ain't no telling how many brods she might have wit' her.

"Yeah, I'm sho'," I told him.

"Cool," Andy replied.

About time we pulled up to the projects, I was knocked out in the back seat. Blue Black had to shake me about three times to wake me up. I gave both of them some dap then Blue Black told me to take my tired ass inside.

After I told Blue Black, "fuck you", I did just what he said and took my ass inside. As soon as I hit the bed, no more than ten seconds later, I went right back to sleep.

# -Chapter 2-

(Monique)

It was 6:00 in the evening and once again Antoine is just waking up. While he showered, I sat in the living room trying to figure out all the possible reasons he would have of staying out all night every night.

"Momma I'm full," Jonathan complained.

"Boy you better eat the rest of that food. Ain't nobody got nothin' for you to be throwing away."

"Awww man," Jonathan continued.

"Aw man my ass!" I raised my voice to let him know I was serious. "Jonathan, sit down right now and finish it."

After Antoine came out the bathroom, I gave him some time to get dressed before I told J.J to go tell him to come here.

When J.J came back, and was back on the floor next to his brother, Antoine was coming out. Antoine started talking before I could even ask him anything. "Monique I already know what you about to say and my bad for not coming back last night. I was...."

I cut him off by holding up the plastic bag with the stuff inside of it. "Can you explain this Antoine?" I watched his eyes fall to the floor in search of an answer. "Come sit down for a minute."

"It's not real Monique." Antoine said, while sitting on the couch beside me.

"I know it's not real, but what are you doing with it?" More silence, as his eyes went back to wondering. "Antoine, talk to me. Why are you staying out all day and half of the night? You don't even bother to come inside to get somethin' to eat. Shit, it's almost like you don't live here. You running around that Greyhound Bus Station selling this stuff to those junkies like none of them won't get mad and try to do you somethin' behind their money."

"Monique ain't nothin' gon' happen to me," Antoine replied.

"That's not the point Antoine. Now why are you staying away so much?"

"I'm just tryin' to keep from getting in your way Monique."

I paused for a second and thought about what he just said before I continued. "Antoine, you're not in my way. I want you to be here, but you never are. Your momma calls all the time asking to speak to you. You never give me the opportunity to say, 'Hold up Angela, let me go get him from out of the kids' room.' When she ask me where you at, I have to lie to my sister and say you just left out just to keep her from worrying herself to death. Antoine, I'm not sure if it's your momma that you mad at or if it's her husband, but what's going on with y'all?"

"Ain't nothin' going on Monique," Antoine answered. "I just didn't wanna live there no more."

We'll, I see he still don't want to talk about what's going on with his momma and the pastor so I just left it alone.

"Momma we finished," J.J said.

"Alright," I responded. "Y'all go put those dishes in the sink then you and your brother get ready to take a bath." J.J and Jonathan both got up and headed for the kitchen. "Make sho' y'all asses ain't leave no food on that floor."

"Antoine, I want you to stop selling this stuff and stay away from that bus station." I told my nephew.

"Ok Monique," Antoine said, "I'ma stop."

"Can you try to be at the house a little more? Antoine it have food in there. Your momma brought some groceries over twice since you been here, but you haven't been around to eat none of it."

Antoine nodded his head then said, "I won't be out so much."

I took a deep breath then told him that that was it. Antoine got up from the sofa and walked toward the front door when I remembered that it was something else I wanted to tell him. "Oh, and one more thing Antoine: Can you watch J.J and Jonathan for me tonight?"

"No problem Monique. What time?" Antoine asked.

"Well, Playboys got a get in free before 10:00 special for ladies on Sunday nights, so we prolly leave at 'round 9 or 9:15."

"Aiight, I'll be back before then." Antoine answered.

"Antoine, you know that's only 2 hours away." I said, doubtin' seriously if he'll be back in time.

"Yea I know," Antoine answered. "I'm just going to Big Mike's house. I'll be back way before 9.

"Alright," I said, still not really believing him.

As Antoine opened the front door to go out, Crystal and Tonya were coming in. While Antoine was passing by them, I noticed him and Tonya staring at each other. The first thing that came to mind was what the fuck she looking at my nephew like that for; that bitch know I'd beat her ass if she try to mess wit'.... No that hoe didn't just smile at him.

"Tonya if you don't stop fuckin' playing wit' me!" I yelled, ready to get off of this couch and whoop that bitch's ass.

"Girl what," Tonya asked, playing dumb founded.

"Girl what my ass," I said, letting her know that I was top of her shit. "I saw the way you and Antoine were smiling at each other. Don't make me beat the shit out of the both of y'all asses."

"Damn, Monique calm down." Crystal said, while sitting on the couch across from me. "Tonya, girl you better stop playin' wit' Monique's nephew."

"Girl don't nobody want your nephew," Tonya said. Trying to make me think that I can turn my back on the two of them and she wouldn't try to do something wit' him. Yea right, I know that hoe too good for me to do some dumb shit like that. "I was just messing wit' him Monique. Trust me, that lil' boy can't do nothin' for me and my bills."

"Well stop fuckin' playing wit' him then!" I screamed.

"Monique, girl you alright," Crystal asked. "Lester still hasn't come home yet huh?"

"That gotta be it," Tonya agreed, as she opened her purse and pulled out a pack of cigarettes, "Bitch screaming at me behind some fucking Antoine."

"Have he called or anything?" Crystal asked.

I reached over to the table beside me and grabbed my pack of Cool's from off of it. "Girl it's been three days now. Last night I called everywhere looking for that boy. I called Earl K. Long Hospital, Lady of the Lake Hospital, Baton Rouge General. He ain't at none of them. I called the parish prison to see if they had him. He not there either."

"Did you try West Baton Rouge?" Crystal asked.

"I tried east and west," I told her. "Plus, earlier today when me and Jonathan was walking to the store, I saw his cousin Joe. Asked him and he said that he haven't seen him in three days either."

"Damn, this don't sound like something that Lester would do." Crystal said, while getting the astray from Tonya.

"And to think, I'm three months pregnant and his ass wanna pull this shit." I took a long drag from the Cool. "I'm not 'bout to let that boy stress me out."

"Fa'real girl, don't let Lester get ya nerves all worked up," Tonya said. "'Cause remember what one nigga won't do, believe me, the next one will be more than happy to do it for him."

"Look at this hoe," Crystal said.

"Yep, and a good hoe too. But I bet you two hoe's be hoeing right on side of me tonight." Tonya said, "Especially you Crystal; with that lil' two piece that you plan on wearing."

"You ain't never lying," Crystal agreed, while slapping hands with Tonya.

"Monique, you should see that lil' two piece this bitch got for tonight. I'm talking 'bout ass and titties everywhere." Tonya said.

"Damn Crystal, Kevin letting you put on something like that?" I asked, while looking at Crystal in shock.

"Let?" Crystal said, like Kevin ass wasn't a psychopath. "Shit, he the one that bought it for me. Kevin knows when the club close that his goodies coming right back home to him."

"Monique, what time your sister said she'll be here?" Tonya asked.

"She said she shouldn't be here no later than 9," I answered. "You know first she gotta wait until Jason start's smoking that weed so he can pass out and she can sneak out without him ever knowing anything; just like she did last time."

"You see, your sister Evet is what I call a badd bitch,"

Tonya said. "Any bitch that got a husband at home and still comes inside at three and four o'clock in the morning is my type of bitch."

The three of us talked for a couple more minutes before Crystal and Tonya left to take a bath and get ready. Since all of us lived in the same building, they were only a few feet away from their place.

The projects down south are different from the ones that I heard about up there in New York City. I heard they have projects as big as fifty floors high. Ours are not like that. The projects in Baton Rouge, and just about everywhere else down south, are no higher than two stories up and spread throughout the city. Every hood in Baton Rouge has at least a few. The project's here on 17$^{th}$ Street is six separated two story buildings with about thirty-five units in each set.

Crystal lived in #114 with her boyfriend Kevin and her three kids, two girls and a boy. Her son Micheal is the same age as J.J so either Micheal is over here playing the PlayStation or J.J and Jonathan are down there with him playing his Super Nintendo. Her lil' girl Doria is the oldest. I think she's 10, and Crystal just had a baby girl in February that she named Jasmine.

Tonya lived two doors down from Crystal, in #116. Tonya has three kids too, but none of them lives with her. They live with their grandparents over in C.C. Lockdown. Tonya's oldest daughter, Treasure, is seven years old. She also has two beautiful twin girls name Mya and Nya that's three. I love having her kids at my place, whenever Tonya does have them, but she only have them every blue moon. Her momma don't like to bring them over here because she say Tonya don't be watching them and she be having all kinds of niggas around them.

I let J.J and Jonathan play their game while I took my bath. Within an hour, I was dressed and ready. I had Jonathan take his bath first so Antoine wouldn't have to worry about him. Last time I went out and left it up to Antoine to bath them, he said that he damn near had to whip Jonathan to get him to get in the tub.

I was on the phone with my sister when Tonya came knocking on the door. After I let her in, I related the message to her that Evet was on her way and went back to putting on my make up in the bathroom. I could hear Tonya in the living room fumbling through my CD collection.

She called out to me and asked, "Monique, where your Trina and Trick Daddy CD at?"

"It's in the CD player in my room," I yelled back.

She went got the CD and put it in big stereo that I had in the living room. Tonya put the track on #5, "Nann." As Tonya started singing along with Trina, she yelled,

"You don't know nann hoe

who tried all type of shit,

who quick to deep throat a dick,

and let another bitch come lick the clit.

No you don't know nann hoe."

~ 35 ~

I started singing the song myself as I looked at my watch and noticed it was already five minutes after nine. I told Jonathan to hurry up and get out that damn tub so his brother could get in, then went in the living room to see has Antoine made it back.

I walked in the living room and saw Crystal on the couch rolling a blunt and Tonya sitting next to her drinking a shot of Gin and Cranberry Juice. Both of them raised their head when I came in.

Tonya started reaching me the bottle of Gin and told me to pour up. Instead of getting the bottle from her, I went and turn down the music.

"Did Antoine come back yet?" I asked.

"Nah uh," Tonya answered. "What time he said he'll be here?"

"I told him to be back before nine and he said alright, and that he was just going to Big Mike's house."

"Have you talked to him about the dummies yet," Crystal asked.

"Yea we talked earlier today. He said he was gonna stop." I told her.

"You think he will?" Tonya asked.

"I don't know," I replied. "He sounded like he was serious, and he said he'll start being around the house more. He still ain't wanna talk about what's going on with his momma and the pastor though."

"Antoine still hasn't told you why he ain't wanna live there no more?" Crystal asked.

"Nope," Right after I said that, Antoine came walking through the door.

"Monique we talked him up." Crystal said.

Antoine came in and asked were we waiting on him. I told him that Evet still ain't come yet. Then he asked if he could have company over.

"Who, a girl," I asked.

"Yea," Antoine answered. "We gon' stay in the living room and watch TV."

"What girl are you talking about bringing here?" I asked, wondering what girl he met over here already.

"Big Mike's cousin, Iesha," Antoine answered.

"Iesha!" Tonya yelled out; just as shocked as I was.

"Ain't that girl about nineteen or twenty years old?" I asked, but knowing she was. Iesha went to the same high school as me and Tonya. I think Iesha was in the ninth grade when we were in the eleventh. "When y'all started liking each other?"

"We just cool Monique." Antoine said, thinking he's talking to a fool. "Ain't nothin' going on betweem us."

I told him, no, and to wait until I'm around before he invite a girl over. We heard a horn repeatedly blowing outside. Crystal already knew who it was, but still went looked out the balcony window before she said that my crazy sister was out there.

I told Antoine that Jonathan had already taken his bath and J.J was in the tub now so the only thing he had to do was make them take their asses to sleep. He said alright while walking me to the door then closing it behind us.

"Y'all bitches dressed to impress huh?" Evet said, as we got in her black Nissan and closed the door. "Crystal, what the hell you got on?"

"Nothin'," Tonya answered for Crystal.

"Girl, Kevin must be in a good mood for him to let you go to the club in something like that." Evet said, looking at all the skin Crystal had showing.

Crystal is 6.6, brow skin with shoulder length hair. A person could never tell that she has three kids just by looking at her body. Tonight, because of the blue jeans Daisy Dukes she was wearing, if you're a man standing below 5.7, the first thing you'll see on her is some long shining brown legs. If you're a man standing above 5.7, the first thing you would see is about three quarters of her double D's showing, because the red tube top she had on wasn't putting up any fight in trying to hide them. Someone could barely bump into her tonight and that tube top would turn into invisible top which would make those three quarters of double D's turn into, dollar dollar bills.

I was surprised myself that Kevin let her put that on. Last year, one night when me and Crystal was going out, Kevin came to my place and called her all kinds of bitches and hoes because of the clothes she was wearing. He said that we wasn't fooling nobody and that we was going to a nigga's house. He ended up jumping on Crystal that night and literally dragging her by the hair back to their place. After about a week of her staying inside, prolly to let her face go down, she came over telling me that Kevin was drunk and that he apologized and told her that he would never do it again. Kevin had already came to my apartment the day before and apologized to me for bringing that bullshit to my house. Me personally, I wouldn't give a fuck how many times a nigga apologized for putting his hands on me. If he ever goes to sleep around me again, I bet his ass never wake up again.

"After I put this head and pussy on him, girl he was asking me if I needed any money to go wit' it." Crystal said.

Bout time we made it to the club, it was five minutes till, and the way it was packed, we knew it'll be well after 10 before we got to the door.

"Damn girl, then we gotta park almost a block away. Whoever is at the door prolly look at us crazy; trying to get in for free." Tonya said, as we all got out the car.

"Girl, I wouldn't give a fuck if it's eleven o'clock when we get there." Evet replied. "I ain't paying shit, and they gon' let us in."

We reached the doorman twenty minutes after, but he ain't trip. The only thing he was worried about was getting Tonya's number. She stayed there and talked to him while we went inside.

Judging by the long line we had to stand in, the inside didn't have as many people as we thought, but it was still pack. We found a table almost in the back by where the niggas that be shooting dice on a pool table be at. I went sat down to make sho' nobody came and took our spot while Evet and Crystal went to the bar and ordered the drinks.

As I looked around, I couldn't help but noticed the difference between here at Playboys and Club Shenanigan's where we went last weekend. To me, Club Shenanigan's is ten times better than here. It's prolly because at Shenanigan's you have to be twenty-one and older to get in. Plus, you can't wear white tees. Here at Playboys it's eighteen and up, come as you are. I know that's not a big difference in the age group, but the "no tee shirt policy" makes a difference in the crowd the club brings and a big difference in your chances of getting through the night without somebody shooting. Only reason I came here is so I could take my mind off of Lester. God I hope ain't nothing happen to him.

"Monique, you ain't tell me what you wanted so I got you what you got last time." Evet said, as she hands me a glass. "Amaretto and pineapple juice, huh?"

I nodded my head up and down and told her, yea.

As she sat in the chair across from me, I noticed Tonya was with them. Tonya held two Budweiser bottles in one hand and a glass in the other. She sat down and put one of the Budweiser in front of me. We stayed there until we were finished with the glasses then we took the beers to the dance floor.

On our way, I noticed just how much the place changed

within the thirty minutes we been here. It went from packed to jam packed. We stood with the crowd around the dance floor and sipped our beers as we watched people dancing to Juvenile's back that ass up. Tonya and Evet went danced first; me and Crystal continue to watch from the side.

"I'm coming back," Crystal yelled over the loud music.

While she went to the bathroom, they had these two chicks on the dance floor dancing their ass off. People started forming a circle around them when two dudes got on the floor and the chicks hit a split on top of them and started bouncing up and down.

It looked like they were really fucking, except they still had on their clothes. I know the dudes had to be rocked up as the chicks grind and rolled all on them.

"I bet chu can do it better." A voice said from behind me.

"I ain't finna try it to find out." I yelled over my shoulder.

"We'll let's start off light then."

I turned around to see how this nigga looked; talking to me.

"Damn" was the word that slipped from out of my mouth. The lights were low so I couldn't really see him that much, but what I couldn't help but see was all of the jewelry he had on. His diamond earrings were the size of mini golf balls and his chain was, diamond-up! I couldn't make out the piece that was on it, but it looked like a dragon or something, and it had red, yellow, and white diamonds shinning off it. I pulled his shades off his eyes so I could get a better look at his face. He flashed me a half of smile to show me his mouth full of gold.

I fixed his glasses back then turned around and wrapped his arm around my waist. He held on tight as I started popping on him hard. We went at it strong for about ten minutes. Then we slowed it down. He kept his arm wrapped around me as we talked.

We exchanged names then he asked me who I came to the club with. I told him, then he asked, "Where your nigga at, ma?"

I simply raised my shoulders up and down. He told me that he was finna go get something to drink and asked if I needed anything. I told him that he could just bring me another Budweiser, and he walked off.

I watched him as he made his way through the crowd, then I noticed Tonya walking off the dance floor with some nigga. She didn't bother to look my way. I continued to watch them until they were out the club.

Evet and Crystal came over wiping the sweat off their face and chest with a paper towel. Crystal leaned toward my ear and asked me if I saw Tonya walking out the club with that nigga?

I nodded my head up and down. Crystal looked at me for a few seconds then shook her head from left to right.

When Lance came back with the beer, I asked him for his cell phone. He gave it to me and I programed my number in it under call me any time tomorrow then hand it back to him. He read it, then nodded his head at me and walked off.

Clap, clap, clap, clap, clap, clap, was all you heard as Tonya bent over on the back seat of Tommy's Toyota 4-Runner. Tommy went to the same high school as us. Him and Tonya use to mess around for a short period. It lasted for, I'd say a month. Then Tommy got word from his friend Leon that Tonya was fucking a nigga that went to school with Leon's cousin.

Tommy confronted her about it and she denied it of course, that is until two weeks later when Leon called Tommy and told him to turn on his computer and go to home video porn.com. Tommy saw it plain and clear for his self. While Tommy watched Tonya on his computer screen riding a dude with the same skills that had him damn near hooked, he felt passed played. He sat there and watched the whole thing still not able to believe that he was seeing his girl like that with somebody else.

When it was almost over, Tommy couldn't hold his stomach any longer. He watched the dude pull out and cum in Tonya's mouth. After Tommy cleaned out his insides, he immediately called Tonya on the phone and called her all kinds of bitches and hoes. He never talked to her again until tonight.

Tommy was a little drunk when he seen Tonya on the dance floor. He looked at her as a quick fuck. He remembered about the video in high school and told Tonya to turn around as he got ready to bust. He came in Tonya's mouth as well. She wrapped her hand around Tommy's man hood as she sucked the head to make sho' she got it all out.

Back in the club, Tonya went and got another beer from the bar and came stood by us like nothing ever happened.

~ 43 ~

-Chapter 3-

(Antoine)

After I made J.J and his brother go in their momma's room and close the door, me and Iesha went in their room. The lights were already off so as soon as I closed the door behind us, Iesha started kissing and licking on my neck. I let her do her thang while I gripped her soft lil' booty through the brown shorts she had on.

Both of us knew her purpose of being here while Monique was at the club so we wasted no time on bullshitting as she started pulling up my shirt. After I helped her take it off, I grabbed her by the ass again and picked her up. Being that I'm not too up on that mouth to mouth stuff, I carried her to the bed, laid her down, and went straight for the section that's been on my mind the most.

I took off her shirt and she took her bra off. I only sucked on her titties for a few seconds before she reached down and started unbuckling my Cowhide Belt. I stood up so that I could take off my Girbaud Jeans and Reeboks Tennis Shoes. By now, my eyes were fully adjusted to the darkness. Iesha kicked off her

Nike Air Max then came out of her shorts and underwear in one quick motion. I walked over to the dresser where I kept my boxers and socks and pulled out three condoms. I hope she wouldn't thinking that I was about to run in her naked headed. If she was, then she must've had me confused with somebody else because Trap been put me on game with that. I threw two condoms on the floor next to the bed then put on the other one and made sho' I pulled it all the way to the base. I quickly climbed back on top of her so that I could hurry up and have her out of here before Monique came back. Even though, I had already decided that if I heard the front door open then Iesha would just have to climb out the window.

When Iesha finally got tired of me trying, she grabbed it and put it in herself. Twenty minutes later, I was finished and Iesha was back fully dressed. I walked her to the projects' park and told her that I was gonna call her later on tonight then I turned back around.

I heard the phone ringing as soon as I got to the front door.

"Hello," I said, reaching the phone on the third ring.

"What up nigga?"

Realizing it was my lil' cousin, Tito, I sat down on the couch and put my feet up on the table. "I'm good cuz." I responded.

My cousin Tito: He's what you would call, a real black sheep of the family. He wasn't allowed at none of our aunties houses because he had a reputation for stealing a lot. Me personally, I think somebody in the family made it up for whatever reason. Everybody else just ran with it. The real reason the family don't like him is because he did some time in L.T.I Juvenile Facility when he was only 10 years old. They got him for shooting a mail lady with a BB gun. Don't get me wrong, ain't nobody perfect. Shit I do all kinds of dirt, but even I wouldn't do that.

I heard the judge had originally sentenced Tito to juvenile life, but he ended up doing a year and a half and came home on probation until he turn twenty-one. When I asked him about it, he told me that he was just target practicing.

Since I moved back on this side, we've been jammed tight. Besides my partner in crimes, Tito is also my partner in rhymes. We're both underground artistes waiting to be discovered. Really and truly, we're just trying to do whatever it takes to get rich. We still haven't dropped a CD yet, or even seen the inside of a studio for that matter, but we will. Until that day comes though, it's get it how you live for us.

"I just got finished smashing this lil' brod that stay over here," I said.

"What lil' brod," Tito asked.

"You don't know her," I said. "She lives on side of the projects. I just walked in from walking her to the park."

"Where Monique at," He asked.

"She at the club," I answered. "Aye Tito, mane you should've seen what her girl Tonya had on tonight."

"What she had on?" Tito asked.

"A white cat suite, and looked like she ain't have on no type on draws underneath. I'm talking 'bout ass jiggling everywhere."

"Damn, I could imagine how she was looking." Tito said, "Tonya fine ass; caramel skin, baby doll face, nice apple size titties, big ass booty, perfect height. Man Tonya badd fa'real. Boy if I was staying with Monique, I'd be trying to hit that every time she came over."

"What you think I'm doing; bullshitting?" I asked. "Tonya knows what's up with me. I think she just scared of Monique."

"What she think Monique will tell her something?" Tito asked.

"Tell her something?" I asked, like that was the craziest question I had ever heard. "Monique'll beat the breaks off of Tonya if she ever found out something happened between us."

"Man Monique needs to chill out with all that," Tito said, while sounding like he was messing with his tape player in the background. "What's been up wit'cha raps though; have you come up wit' anything lately?"

"Nah uh," I answered. "I've been in them streets chasing paper."

"Damn Toine, you tripping. I've been coming up with all kinds of stuff. I came up with this one course that I want you to write something to."

"Aiight," I said. "Let me hear it?"

After Tito got finished rapping the course to me, he put in his C-Murder tape and put it on Master P and C-Murder's, "This one for my lil' niggas".

I told him, "Cool, I got it."

He replied telling me to call him when I'm finished.


Thirty minutes later, I called him back with my verse.  He told me to hold on a minute and put the phone by the radio so I could hear the beat then he went picked up another phone so he could listen.

After I spit my verse to him, we stayed on the phone for a few more minutes.  We ended the call with him saying that he'll be over here tomorrow.


THE NEXT DAY:

Standing on the corner in the summer time for hours without anything happening, sometimes made you feel like getting a nine to five may not be such a bad idea.  Until you remember that you're only thirteen years old.

I stood there in my white t-shirt, blue Girbaud, and all black Soulja Reebok's.  The lil' chic in the project's that usually brad my hair told me to come back after 3:00 and she would take care of me.  Until then, I had to play a fro, which made my dark skin turn 3 shades darker in all this heat.  I kept my eyes traveling to all four ends of the streets, thinking, "Where the hell is all the junkies?"

I started pacing back and forth on the corner when I noticed an old school Bonneville driving slowly toward me.  The car passed me by, but then it made the block back around.  I watched as C.J, also known as Big Thug, pulled in front of me and got out.

"What's up lil' one," Big Thug asked, now standing within arm reach.

"Tryin' to get it," I answered.

Big Thug went in his pockets and pulled out a pack of Camel Hump.  He took a cigarette out of the nearly fresh pack and lit it.  "Yea, I see you trying, but you trying the wrong way lil' one.  Selling dummies is not the way to go about getting money.  Me personally, I ain't tripping on you 'cause you not affecting my bread.  All my people know to deal with me and only me.  I'ma tell you like a man though, one of them junkies gonna end up doing you something behind their money.  Then, you know that if the cops catch you with that stuff they gon' charge you like its real.  All this time I been seeing you out chea you should be ready to score you something by now?"

"I don't know," I told him.  "I ain't never talked to anyone about it."

"What chu want; a gram, a sixteenth, a ball?"  Big Thug asked.

Shit, I never even heard of a ball before. I heard of a sixteenth through Andy and I knew that it cost sixty dollars. A gram sounded like something more suitable for me, being that I never had any real dope before. "Give me a lil' second," I said. "I'ma let chu know."

Big Thug told me that I can get a gram from him for thirty-five dollars and make sixty to seventy off it. I nodded my head at him then his cell phone started ringing. He answered it then turned back around and got in his car.

I stood there for a couple of moments and thought about what he said. To have some real dope would feel good. I wouldn't have to worry about selling only to junkies that don't know me, while the ones that do, see me and walk the other way. I'd be able to serv'em all.

On the other hand, why should I spend money to make money. If I score a gram for 35.00, he said I would make a twenty-five to thirty-five dollar profit. I could just continue with these dummies and make all profit; something from nothing. With the real dope, I'll be able to get a rental like Andy did. I debated with myself for another moment.

I probably end up scoring something from him later on, but for right now, I like the sound of, "All Profit."

Since wasn't anything coming through, I headed back to the project's. "I'll be back tonight."

When I walked through the door, Monique was sitting in

the living room smoking a cigarette. "Antoine, you came just in time." Monique said, stopping me before I went in the room. "I wanted to go to the store and I ain't felt like putting some clothes on Jonathan.

"Aiight," I said, and continued walking.

"Antoine, what you plan on doing about school?" Monique asked. "You know it's about to start back in two weeks."

"I'ma transfer to McKinley Middle," I said.

"Don't you need your momma for that?" Monique asked, looking confused.

"Nah uh, I can transfer myself."

"How you gon' transfer yourself," Monique asked, knowing damn well that I couldn't.

"All I have to do is go to the principal's office and tell him that I wanna transfer schools. My momma don't have to sign anything so they not gon' trip."

"Oh, alright," Monique said. Monique may have let it go, but I could tell that she wasn't buying it. "Well, I'm just going to the store."

...................................................................................

After Monique paid for her a fresh pack of Cool's, Laze Potato Chips, and a cold drink, she walked out of the store and saw Lester cousin Joe standing outside. Joe was with three dudes, but when he saw Monique he broke off from the group and started walking towards her.

"Got bad news for you ma," Joe approached Monique with a sad look on his face. "Our boy Lester is in jail."

"What jail is he in," Monique asked, "'Cause I've called everywhere looking for him."

"He called me yesterday and told me to tell you that he's locked up in Mississippi," Joe answered.

"What he doing in Mississippi?"

"I don't know," Joe answered with an easy lie. "He didn't tell me that part. I guess he ain't wanna talk through that phone in jail; you know they listen to every call. He said that he been trying to call you."

"Shit, I can't accept collect calls on my phone." Monique said.

"He told me already," Joe said. "Look, I want you to call the phone company and put it to where you can accept his calls. Don't worry about the bill. I'ma take care of it."

"Ok," Monique said. "Did he tell you if he seen a judge yet or what they charged he with?"

"He said something 'bout he was with Carl and Troy and the cops pulled them over and found a gun in the car. But look, call the phone company, hook that up, and he gon' call you and let chu know what's up."

"Alright then; thank you too Joe," Monique said and was about to turn around.

"Hold up a minute ma," Joe said, then reached down in his pocket and pulled out a knot of money. He peeled off two crispy one hundred dollar bills and hand it to her. "Let me know if you need anything else."

Monique thanked him for the money then went home.


Lester, Carl, and Troy were originally on their way to Biloxi, Mississippi to meet up with a connect that Troy had been telling them about. Before they were able to pick up the two kilos of cocaine, they had to pass through a real country town that was right outside of the Bay Area. A couple of on duty police officers see's three black men at a gas station get into a car that had a Louisiana tag in the back window. Lester didn't want to stop in the first place, but he figured if they were to stop, then it might as well be now because it was no way they were stopping with the drugs in the car.

Being the usual racist dick heads that the cops were known for throughout this part, decides to pull'em over. The cops reason was, let the cops tell it, improper lane switching. Well Lester, Carl, and Troy each have a gun on them. Ain't no way they're pulling over in red neck county. They put the cops on a high speed chase and with Carl's driving skills, they almost got away. Unfortunately none of them noticed the cop up the road from them hiding in the bushes waiting to shoot out their tires, which almost cost them their lives.

The car flipped over in a ditch. Luckily they were able to evaporate before the gas that was leaking from the gas tank could ignite. The three goes to jail and found out the following morning that they were being held without bond. The judge told'em since none of them lived in Mississippi that they were considered a flight risk.

-Chapter 4-

(Antoine)

As it started to get dark, I changed clothes and put on a pair black Girbaud pants with a black t-shirt then laced up the black Reeboks. After standing outside in front of the project's for about fifteen minutes, I saw someone walking toward me In all black too.

"Toine, what's up cuz?"

As me and Tito dapped each other down, I said, "What up gangsta?" We started walking toward the bus station.

We got on Convention Street and Tito pulled out a .38 special. "Look at this bitch. This my momma shit. I took it out of the house while she's at work." Tito gave the gun to me and told me to give him mine's. He said the .38 was too big for him and that he didn't wanna take a chance in the gun going off and shooting somebody or maybe his self.

"Good thinking," I told him.

We sat on the porch across the street from the bus station, at a junkie house I met through Andy, and came up with a game plan.

"Say Toine, you ever robbed a cab before?" Tito asked.

"Other than for a ride, no," I responded. "You think they be having a lot of money on'em?"

"Hell yeah, them bitches got to," Tito answered. "Look at how much they be costing. They make at least twenty-five to fifty dollars for damn near every ride. Then they do that shit all day long. I know for a fact those mother fuckers got money on'em."

"Let's go check it out then," I said. We stood up and walked across the street.

We jumped in one of the Yellow Smith's Cabs that was sitting in front of the bus station. Shit, Yellow Smith starts their needles off at $3.85 alone. Since they charge the most, we knew at the end of the day, they would most likely have the most.

I told the driver to take us to Sherwood. Sherwood is on the other side of town. I told him to take us there because I wanted to throw him off and make him think that we lived somewhere around that area. When we got there, Tito led him down a few dark streets.

"You could stop here," I said. I didn't know where the hell we were, but I didn't want him to keep driving until he was on to us and came up with a plan.

The cab driver pointed to one of the houses that he stopped in front of and asked, "Is this the house?"

"Say gangsta, this where she stay at huh," I asked Tito.

"Yea this it," Tito answered, then pointed the broke .25 at the cab driver's head. I had Tito's momma's .38 special already out, so together we said, "Give it up bitch!"

The fat white man quickly put up his hands and said, "I don't have anything."

"Bitch stop lying," Tito said, then slapped the man in the head with the broke .25.

I reached over the front seat and went in his front two pockets. I only found four twenties, a ten, and a five dollar bill. "Bitch where the rest of the money at?"

"I don't," Were the only words the cab driver got to say, before Tito slapped him with the pistol again.

As blood started oozing from the man's mouth, I noticed a tear drop coming down his check.

"Come on gangsta," I told Tito. "Let's get up out of here. This mother fucker ain't got nothin'."

I got a chance to get all the way out of the cab, but Tito was a little too slow. Only half of his body was out of the door when the cab driver smashed the gas and almost ran over Tito's legs. Tito rolled on the ground a couple of times before he got up and we both took off running.

We ran until we were a safe distant away from the spot where we got out the cab at, then Tito told me to give him some of the money. I went in my pocket and pulled out two of the twenties and the five dollar bill. All of a sudden, as I was putting the money in Tito's hand, a light shinned in our face. We both turned our heads and seen a police car sitting at the corner.

Tito started running one way and I took off in the other direction. I stayed on the same road until I ran into a big fence that looked to be some apartments behind it. I heard the cop hitting his brakes as soon as I jumped on the gate. I guess his donut eating ass couldn't jump it like I did. After I landed, I looked behind me and he was peeling off in the other direction.

I had on a plain white shirt under the back one so after I took off the black shirt, I pulled out the .38 special and wrapped it inside of the shirt. I walked from behind the apartments and put the shirt in the dumpster. I didn't know where the hell I was, but after I walked all the way into the apartments, I saw nothing but black folks walking around everywhere.

As I began to smile, I said to myself, "I'm in the hood."

I tried to approach the first female that I seen walking by herself, but when she spotted me walking toward her and calling out for her to hold up a minute, she started walking the other way.

"What the fuck she walked away for?" I said to myself. "I know I ain't no ugly ass nigga."

I realized the cops should be here soon so I had to hurry up and do something. I looked around and saw a dude standing by his self in front of an apartment door. He was upstairs leaning over the railing. I walked over to him and asked him from downstairs if I could use his telephone right quick.

He told me to hold on for a minute then turned around and went inside the apartment. On my way to meet him with the phone I noticed a group of people sitting on the stairs. After I stepped through the crowd and was almost at the dude's apartment, he was coming back outside with the cordless phone in his hand.

"Appreciate it gangsta," I said, as he hand me the phone.

"I'ma be over here when you get finished." He said, while using his head to point towards the stairs.

I nodded my head in return then I followed behind him. He walked down the steps to one of the dudes standing up. I sat on the steps as close to the group as I could and called my brother. As I dialed his number, a police car pulled right in front of us and shinned his light in our faces. I held up my right arm to block the light from my eyes while holding the phone to my ear with my other hand. The cop stayed there for a couple of minutes looking at each one of us. Then he pulled off. I started back dialing my brother's number. When Trap picked up the phone, I asked the dude sitting in front of me for this address.

"5123 Brandywine," He said, then turned back around.

I told my brother the address the dude gave me and he said that he knew exactly where that was and that he was on his way. I hung up with him, but because I wanted to make sure the cop were gone, I called this lil' chick name Conseption that I had been talking on the phone with.

I met Conseption when me and my cousin Coon was over in Lake Side about a month ago. Seppy, short for Conseption, was only thirteen years old like me, and she was built like an amazon. She lived on the Lake with her grandmother, and when I say grams were strict, that's an understatement. Grams was, "put that belt on Seppy's ass" strict. Even though grams would watch Seppy's every move, Seppy still could hardly come outside, so it was just a conversational thang with us.

We talked for a few minutes then I told Seppy that I would call her when I got home. She said ok before I hung up with her and went took ole boy back his phone. I told him appreciate it again and he replied by nodding his head then I started walking to the front of the building.

About time I made it to the entrance gate, Trap was coming through it in my momma's 626 Mazda.

"Right on time," I said to myself.

I got in and explained to my brother what happened. After we went got my auntie's gun from out of the dumpster, we drove around looking for Tito. We must've road around Sherwood for over thirty minutes, before Trap said that he had to take momma back her car before she woke up and realized her keys missing. I told him that he could go ahead and drop me off by the projects then.

"You alright huh lil' brother," Trap asked me as he pulled into the projects' parking lot. "You need anything?"

"Nah, I'm good," I told him.

"Aiight. If you ever need something, let me know." Trap said, while putting out his fist to me.

"Fa'shanks," I said, as I dapped him down and got out.

When I got inside, I noticed Monique and Jon-Jon sitting

in the living room.  I spoke to them both then Monique told me that Tito called two times for me.

"How long that's been?" I asked.

"He just called about five minutes ago." Monique answered.

Well at least I know that he ain't get caught.  I thought to myself, and went in the room.  It took Tito maybe 10 minutes before he called again.

"It's for you, Antoine," Monique called out to me.

I went to get the phone from her and she told me to get the cordless phone from out of her room.

"Hello," I said, as I took the cordless phone in J.J's room and closed the door behind me.

"How in the hell you got back?"  Tito asked; sounding pissed off.

"I called Trap to come pick me up," I said.  "Shit, we drove around looking for you for damn near an hour.  Where you at anyway?"

"I'm on Florida Street at the payphone in front of Circle K." Tito answered.  "Where Trap at now?"

"He busted out," I said.  "He had to hurry up and take my momma back her car."

"Where that gun at Toine?  Man, I gotta get that gun back before my momma comes home."

"I got it right here," I said, "Ain't nothin' gon' happen to it."

"Man fa'real Toine. My momma would beat the fuck outta me if she found out I took her gun out the house." Tito said, panicking at the thought of his momma standing over him with a belt or a switch. Knowing his momma Jackie, she prolly would use a broom stick.

"Man quit tripping. You know I ain't gonna let nothing happen to your momma's gun." I said, trying to put his mind at ease.

"Fa'real Toine. I'ma be over there tomorrow."

"What time," I asked.

"Sometime in the morning," Tito answered.

"Aiight. How you plan on getting back to Glen Oaks?"

"I don't even know," Tito answered. "I prolly end up jacking a cab for a ride."

"Fuck no! I know that you can find somebody to call."

"I'ma think of somethin'," Tito told me, then said he out.

I told him aiight then we both hung up.

I didn't really worry too much about how Tito would get home, wasn't anything I could do about it anyway. And when he told me that he would think of something, I knew he'll be straight. Since it was only 10:00, I went chilled over by Big Mike's house.

## -Chapter 5-

(Antoine)

Getting Sherwood middle to drop me from their attendance sheet was a piece of cake. I knew that wouldn't be too hard anyway. When I went in the office and told'em that I was transferring schools, the secretary looked like she had a smile on her face as she gave me my drop slip. I guess that's from all the stuff that I was getting into last year.

On the other hand, Enrolling in McKinley was a different story. I told the principal that my momma wouldn't be able to come to the school because she was sick. I even told him that he could call her and she'll verify everything for him. He wasn't trying to hear it. He said that he couldn't enroll me without her being there. But being that I did say she was sick, he allowed me to attend school for one week. To give her some time to get well. After Friday, she would have to come down to the school with me before I could come back.

1st DAY (Monday):

Yeeeeaaaa! This is the school I supposed to be going to. I

know everybody here. Everybody that I went to school with the year before last is here. Damn near everybody I went to elementary school with is at this bitch. I took a couple classes with my dog Fred so he's the one that showed me around. I knew Fred from elementary school. Me, him, and his lil' sister Inez went to Dufrocq together. Plus, they go to Pastor Franklin's church too so we've been jam tight for years now.

When Fred first showed me to my forth hour class, out the gate, I knew it would be my livest hour. The teacher was writing something on the chalkboard while the students were sitting on the desk, throwing paper across the room, and doing everything but listening to what he was saying. Me and Fred went sat in the back.

"Say Toine, you remember that lil' brod Erica over there?" Fred asked.

I looked in the direction that Fred was looking in. "Nah uh," I said, after a few seconds of studying her face. "Who she is?"

"She went to elementary school with us too," Fred answered.

"Oh," I responded, still not remembering her. "Aye, what my momma them been up to?"

"Same old, chilling," Fred responded. "Oh, I knew it was somethin' I had to tell you. Mane bruh, your brother just went put two more in his mouth."

"You bullshitting," I quickly said, not believing that Trap had gotten some more gold teeth. "I just saw that nigga 'bout two weeks ago."

"He must've just gotten them Friday or Saturday, 'cause I ain't see them in his mouth Thursday.  Yesterday at church I saw them as clear as day, two at the top and two at the bottom."

2$^{nd}$ Day (TUESDAY):

"What's up roune?"  I asked Fred, as we approached each other that morning.  "Boy you look like you're still sleep.  Wipe the crust out cha eyes."

"Shit, I am still sleep."  Fred responded, as we stood in the middle of the hallway.  "I ain't felt like coming to this bitch no."

Me and Fred went stood against the wall and waited for the bell to ring for us to go to first hour.

"Aye Fred, I thought that bitch ass nigga Peter go here."

"I knew it, I knew it, I knew it."  Fred emphasized his words by punching his fist in his hand.  "You gon' beat that nigga up huh?"

"Come on Fred," I paused and looked at Fred in the eyes. "You should already know what's up with me."

"Aye look, that nigga suspended right now, but he'll be back on Thursday." Fred responded.  "Stupid ass got suspended for three days from cussing out his third hour teacher, Ms. Stinner."

The bell ringed so me and Fred dapped each other down. He told me that he would holla at me next hour.

Peter White. I guess you can say that he's an old friend of mine. Growing up, we used to run together hard. We used to go to Wal-Mart together to steal reflectors for our bikes, sneak in the movie theatre together without paying, beat people up at school together. You know, we did everything that normal kids our age are supposed to do. Then all of a sudden, when I moved from out the south and transferred schools, he started going around telling people that I used to wear his clothes all the time, jock his style, always following up behind him, and just saying a lot of brod type shit. Everybody knew he was lying 'cause I dressed ten times better than him when you compared my worst days to his best. Still and all, it's only mandatory that I check the clown and see what's up with him.

3<sup>rd</sup> Day (WEDNESDAY):

"Antoine, where you been all this time," Latoya asked.

"I been in ghost town," I answered. "My people them decided to move over on North Foster. I've been going to Sherwood Middle." Latoya was a lil' chick that I was trying to get on at South East Middle. When I say lil' momma was badd, mane, she was cold bloody; pretty face with a coke bottle shape. We took the same fifth hour class together. "So what's up with us ma?" I said, switching the subject to what's really good. "Are we gonna pick back up from where we left off?"

"Where we left off at?" Latoya asked. Looking at me like she was dumb founded.

"Come on Toya; don't play crazy."

"Antoine, wasn't you messing with Keisha Earns at South East?"

"Nah uh, me and that girl ain't mess around. I wouldn't try to mess with her and you at the same time."

"Yea right," Latoya said, messing up my game mode, "And by now you prolly already got one of these chicken heads around here."

I was too into trying to get the ball back rolling with Latoya to notice Jazz Shepherd come sit in the desk behind me. He tapped me on my shoulder to get my attention, "Aye Toine, you know your boy Pet come back to school tomorrow huh; you gon' fight him?"

"Damn, who told him?" I thought to myself and then wondered who else knew?

4$^{th}$ Day (Thursday):

The first hour bell had just started ringing when I got to school. As soon as I walked through the front door, I bumped dead into the principal.

"Mr. Guillard, just the person I needed to see." Mr. Jones said. "Come on in my office."

"Shit," I said to myself, as I put my head down and followed behind him. When we got in his office, he told me to have a sit. Then he went sat at his desk and stared straight into my eyes without saying anything.

"What's going on Mr. Jones," I asked, trying to break the silent scrutiny.

"What's this I hear about you and Peter White supposed to be fighting?"

"Me and Peter White," I asked, with a puzzled look on my face.

"You do know who he is, right?" Mr. Jones asked.

I knew damn well Mr. Jones knew that I knew who Peter White was. "Yea, I know who he is." I answered, still with the puzzled look. "I thought that we were cool."

"So you didn't come here to fight him?" Mr. Jones pressed.

"Nah uh," I answered, while shaking my head from left to right.

Mr. Jones leaned back in his chair. "When Miss. Guillard coming down here?"

"Oh, she said she'll be here tomorrow." I answered.

After nodding his head up and down, he pointed his index finger at me and said, "Don't come back tomorrow without her."

"Yes sir," I replied.

In my fourth hour class, I told Fred about what happened in the principal's office.

"One of his boys must've went back and told him that you came here to beat him up." Fred said, "That hoe ass nigga prolly had his momma to call up here and talk to the principal. I bet that's why he ain't come to school today."


FRIDAY:

I stood at the far end of the wall that morning trying to make sho' that if the principal passed then I'll have enough time to duck off without him seeing me. I found out that Pet was in the same first hour class as me, so I knew that if he came to school today, then we had to see each other.

I've been standing here for over twenty minutes now and still no sign from neither one. I was starting to think the coward really was hiding from me and decided to stay home again. Then as I continued to watch the front door, I noticed him and two dudes walking through it. When he came to where he could see me, we made eye contact. He stopped, turned my way, then took his book sack off and dropped it on the floor.

"Be cool. Not now." I told him, "We gon' see each other later."

He said a few slick words to me then walked off with his two goons. I guess he thought he did something. The bell ringed so I hurried and went to class.

Fred's lil' sister, Inez, also took the same first hour class as us. When she walked in and saw me sitting at my desk, she started smiling. She already knew what was up. I smiled back at her.

~ 69 ~

Being the last one to come to class, Peter finally walked in. He was still with his two boys from earlier. All three of them stopped at the door and looked at me. Peter turned around and exchanged a few words with them. After their small talk, they gave each other some dap. Peter then turned back around and went sat at his desk. His goons went to their first hour classes.

The intercom came on for the pledge of allegiance so everyone stood up. The teacher was the only one in the classroom to bow her head for the moment of silence. The teacher had the desks set up where half of them were on one side of the class room and the other half was on the other side, facing each other.   Peter desk was directly across from mine so all of the students watched me and Peter, as we stared each other down.

"Bitch ass nigga, what the fuck you looking at?" I asked. The class remained silent. "Boy you better take ya eyes off me before I come over there and beat the fuck out chu."

I started walking towards him.  His crazy ass waited till I was a few feet away from him to try and take off his shirt. As soon as he got it over his head, I hit him with three quick hard punches to both sides of his face. He stumbled back, but kept his balance. We went at it, punch for punch, lick for lick. It lasted for the better half of a minute, which I'd say is about seventy something punches coming from each party. Then, either his arms died out or his face couldn't take it no more. He hurried up and grabbed me.

"Nah uh, bitch ass nigga don't hold me now." I said, trying to unwrap his arms from around me.

A few of the students came and grabbed me; some grabbed him. One of the teachers from down the hall came and took Peter out the classroom.

The principal came in. "This boy doesn't even go to school here. You're trespassing."

"Shit," I said aloud, and walked out with Mr. Jones.

When we got by his office which was by the front door of the school sounded like I could hear the sunlight calling my name. Mr. Jones must be crazy if he thinks I'm about to sit around and wait for the cops to come pick me up. I struck out running through the front door and didn't stop until I was two blocks away.

My cousin, Coon, lived not too far from McKinley Middle so I went to his house. Coon was a few years older than me, but he dropped out of school a few years back and his momma works in the morning, so I knew his house would be a good spot for me to chill at.

We were in his room bumping his new Makaveli CD when the phone ringed. Coon looked at the caller ID box and seen that it was our grandma. At first Coon wasn't gonna answer it, but then he told me, "I'ma just tell her that I haven't seen you today."

"Cool," I replied.

After they hung up, Coon related to me, "She said the cops were looking for you and if you run then you'll only make it worst. She told me if I see you, to have you come over to her house. She said they not gon' arrest you; they gon' just write you a summit to come to court."

My grandma lived on Myrtle Street, which was not too far from here; walking distant. After I debated for a few minutes with Coon, I went ahead and took that walk.

I got on my grandma street and noticed her sitting outside on the porch. When she saw me walking toward the house, she began dialing numbers on her cordless phone. I sat down on the steps and waited for them to come. The cops must've been somewhere in the area because no more than three minutes after she hung up, a police car pulled up to the house. The cop did exactly what Coon told me she said they'll do. He wrote me a summit to come to court then left.

My grandma didn't lecture me like I thought she would. She just sat there without saying anything. When she got up and went inside, I got up and walked back to the projects.

## -Chapter 6-

(Monique)

I could hear my phone constantly ringing, but I was too tired to reach over and get it from off of the night stand. It stopped, and started right back again.

"Hello," I said into the phone, still half sleep.

"You have a collect call from, 'Lester', a Gulf Port County Prison Inmate. To accept the charges dial 0. To decline, press 1."

I pressed 0 before the operator could continue. "Hello," I said again.

"Damn woman, you still sleep?" Lester asked.

"Boy you know I don't get up till after 12," I answered.

"Well don't you think that it's about time for you to change your sleeping schedule for when the baby come?"

"The baby'll be alright," I said, then got back comfortable in the bed. "So why you ain't call back last night?"

"'Cause the game had come on," Lester answered. "You know it was the Saints first game of the season and that damn Mike Ditka fucking up already; lost to those sorry ass Falcons. But aye, I talked to my lawyer this morning."

"Did he give us some good news?"

"Mostly everything I already knew. He said that he talked to my probation officer and they told him that if I don't beat this pistol charge then they'll have to violate me."

"After all the money you pay'em every month, can they do that?"

"Yea, that uncle Tom mother fucker could. In that probation agreement I signed, I'm not supposed to pick up any new charges until the three years are up."

"So if you don't beat the gun charge, how much time you think you'll have to do?"

"Off the three years papers, I'ma do one third of it; a year." Lester answered. "And even if I don't beat the pistol charge, simple possession don't carry any real time. The longest they could hold me in here is six months, at the most."

"What days are y'all visitations on?" I asked.

"I think it's on Mondays, but you ain't gotta get Evet to bring you all the way out chea. You could just wait until they ship me to the parish."

"You sho'," I asked.

"Yea, I'm sho' ma," Lester answered. "You need to take you some driving classes anyway. If you get your license, you wouldn't have to worry about finding a ride."

"I probably think about taking some after the baby come."

I told him.

"Yea right, you know how many times you said that you'll think about it?"

"Fa'real Lester. I'ma take some after I have the baby?"

"Aiight ma. I'ma hold you to that too." Lester said, meaning every word.

The operator came on warning us of our one minute remaining. Lester told me that he was about to go to rec and he'll call me back later on. We said our goodbyes and I love yous then hung up. I put the phone back on the night stand, turned over, and went back to sleep.

Not too long after, the phone went back to ringing again.

"Hello."

"Monique, you still sleep? Girl, get out that damn bed! It's going on one o'clock and ya ass is still laying down."

"Good morning momma," I said, hearing the sound of my momma's usual cheerful voice. My momma, known to everyone else in the hood as Gramma Sweets, was 57 years old with two gold teeth in the front of her mouth and has prolly been the biggest hustler in South Baton Rouge since the late 70's. My momma never sold any drugs or anything, not that I know of, but she has sold everything that was considered legal. My momma Sweets was the one that sold all the dope boys around here their first old school. My momma sold the best pecan candy in town, all year round. She sold TV's, furniture, dogs, just about whatever you could think of that's legal she sold. She also held a tonk game three nights a week at her house. And still today, she's the only person that ever fell with 31 and got away with it.

"Look at'cha. I said its 1:00 and you still hollering 'bout some good morning. You know that boy got put outta school today, huh?"

"Who, Antoine," I ask.

"Who else? You know I ain't talkin' 'bout J.J. The cops came here this morning looking for him."

"Shhhiiit, what he did this time?"

"Dun beat up some boy over there at McKinley. The cops say that he wouldn't even suppose to be there."

"Have the cops found him yet?"

"Yea," my momma answered. "He came over here and turned his self in. He lucky they ain't take his ass to jail. They just charged him with simple battery and trespassing. He goes to court next month on the twenty-third. Monique, you know what chu gotta do, huh?"

"Yea, I know momma."

"Make him take his ass home Monique. That boy doing anything he wanna do over there. You should've put his ass out when you found that stuff in them kids' room. Now he dun went and gotten expelled from school, and I bet he's still coming inside at two and three o'clock in the morning."

"Hold up momma. That's one thing I can say about him. Ever since we had that talk, he's been coming in at a decent time."

"Monique, listen to me.  Make that boy go home."

"Momma I'm not good at that kind of stuff," I whined.
"You tell him."

"Put him on the phone."  My momma said, sounding a
little too anxious.

"He not here right now."

"Look at that, he left here at 10:00 this morning and he
still ain't been over there yet."

"Momma, what if he won't listen to you when you tell
him?  What if he just be out there running the streets and never
go home?"

"He'll take his ass home.  If not, then his momma and the
pastor won't let him just live out in the streets; they gon' do
something."

"Aye mom, I need to come over there and wash some
clothes."

"At what time?"

"Some time later on.  I'ma have Trish to bring me over
there when she get off work."

"Alright, Shit it's not like I'm going somewhere so come on
when you get ready."

"Alright."

"Call me when Antoine get there."

"Alright momma," I replied.

After we hung up, I went ahead and pulled myself outta bed.


LATER ON THAT EVEVING, while me and the girls were at my place:

"So you and Jon-Jon 'bout to get back together huh," Crystal asked me.

"Hell no," I answered. "Just because I slipped and had sex with him last night doesn't mean we're getting back together."

"Oh, so the sex was a mistake and it won't happen again, right?" Tonya asked.

"I ain't saying all that," I corrected her. "Jon-Jon knows about Lester. I told him and Lance." Lance is the guy that I met at Playboys that night. "Both of them know that whatever we do is just temporary until my man comes home."

"What's going on with Mr. Lance anyway?" Crystal asked, "How the two of y'all been getting alone?"

"Well we haven't fucked; if that's what chu asking."

"I'm not asking all that Monique. I just wanted to know how you and the handsome brother been doing lately."

"Uhm hu," I made that noise to let Crystal know that she

wasn't fooling nobody. "I still haven't seen him since that night at the club. I think he's scared to come in the projects. He always mentioning how niggas be getting robbed over here and stuff."

"Girl he better park that pretty lil' Lexus and get one of them crack head cars over there," Tonya said.

"Shit, being that he not from around here, he should be more worried about getting killed than getting robbed." Crystal stopped talking when she heard the front door open.

Antoine walked in and went straight in the kids' room. I picked up the phone and called my momma.

"Antoine," I yelled out. I was sitting at the bar on the living room side so when Antoine came, I told him to go in the kitchen and I was gonna hand him the phone over the counter; that way he could have a lil' privacy. Me and the girls went back to talking, but we tried to keep it low so Antoine could hear.

We got completely quiet when he said, "I ain't going back grandma." And it sounded like he was crying.

We continued to listen, but Antoine didn't say much after that. He just held the phone and sniffed occasionally. When Antoine was finished, he sat the phone down on the counter and walked out the front door. I picked it up to see if my momma was still on it.

"Hello," I said.

"Yea," my momma responded in a depressing tone.

"Were you still talking to him," I asked.

"I told him to put chu back on the phone."

"Oh, because he just sat the phone down and walked out without telling me nothing. Did he say he was going back home?"

"He said he was."

"Momma you and I both know that boy ain't finna go home."

"Let's hope he does."

......................................................................................

Well, just like we thought, Antoine didn't go home. Matter of fact, it's been three days now and he haven't been to sleep either. All the smokers around the bus station knew him and what kind of product he had so none of them did any business with him. Each day, survival became harder and harder for Antoine. He tried to keep up with his appearance and his hygiene by going in the bathroom at the bus station and taking a quick bird bath. He still had a few dollars in his pocket that he had when he left my place, but between food and the cigarette habit that he picked up within three days his money was running out fast.

Antoine stood on Convention Street until he could no longer take the heat coming from the fire ball in the sky, then he went sat down on the porch of an abandon house. The lady that lived next door from the abandon house was sitting on her porch as well, talking to her friend that lived up the street.

"Girl, that boy homeless," Keisha said. "I see that boy out here all day and night. I wonder where his momma at."

"I see him all the time too," her friend Patty from up the street agreed. "Look at him! Girl that boy finna go to sleep. He can't even keep his eyes open."

"Girl that don't make no sense."

Antoine heard everything the two ladies said about him, but it's not like they were whispering so he wouldn't. After Antoine got tired of dropping his head, which seemed like it weighed sixty pounds, he stood up, told his self he had enough, and started walking to the bus terminate so he could catch the city bus.

The bus terminate wasn't far at all from where he was. It was right up Convention Street. When Antoine made it there, he had to remain walking around. He knew that if he sat down and waited on his bus to come that he would fall asleep and miss it. Antoine eyes were so heavy that when the buses did come, he didn't know which one was his. He had to literally walk all the way up to five buses before he could see the one with the big North Foster sign on it.

It was only 1:00 pm so the buses weren't packed yet. Everybody was either at work or at school. It was only Antoine, a lady with a few grocery bags, and an old man on the North Foster bus. Antoine stood at the back and held on to the railing while he waited for his stop to come.

The bus dropped him off a block away from his momma and the pastor's townhouse apartment. He had to walk the rest.

When he got there, he saw both of their cars parked in their assigned parking spaces. Antoine cursed to his self and continued to hope the pastor wasn't there. "Damn I need some sleep."

When Antoine knocked on the door, his momma answered it. Antoine spoke and waited for her to let him in. After a few moments, Angela moved to the side and pointed to the couch for Antoine to sit down. She then closed the door behind them and went sat on the other couch. Antoine stayed quiet as he watched his momma stare at the blank TV screen.

"Antoine, you know Pastor Franklin mad at you." Angela waited a couple of seconds before she continued. "I can't believe you talked to him like that."

"I'ma apologize to him momma." Antoine replied.

Angela took a deep breath. "He's out of town right now Antoine. You have to wait and talk to him first before you could come back."

As soon as Angela said that, she looked at Antoine and seen how quickly his face expression changed. "Hold up a minute," Angela said, and fast walked back to her bedroom.

When she came back, Antoine was gone and the front door was left open. Angela rushed outside, but didn't see Antoine anywhere. Knowing that he couldn't have left that fast, she called Lashey to come downstairs.

Antoine was sitting on the steps waiting for his momma to go back inside so he could leave without her seeing him. But when he heard her calling for Lashey, he knew that Lashey would easily find him.

"Go give this to your brother," Angela said, and gave Lashey a hundred dollar bill.

Antoine had gotten up from the steps already when he heard Lashey calling his name. When he got in the parking lot, in the opening, Lashey and Angela both began calling out to him.

"Antoine!"

"Antoine!"

"Brother!"

"Antoine!"

After a few calls, Antoine stopped walking and turned around, but he couldn't see anything. This time it wasn't because of the sleepiness he felt, it was because of the tears pouring down his face. Until now, Antoine had never known what it felt like to be alone. He couldn't believe Angela told him that he couldn't come home. Antoine felt betrayed and unwanted.

When he came to North Foster, which is a four-lane and usually busy street around this time, he didn't look to see if a car was coming; didn't care. God had to be on his side that day, because he made it safely across. Antoine didn't bother to wait on the city bus to come. Instead, he walked back to the Greyhound Bus Station.

LATER THAT NIGHT, Antoine and Blue Black were together. Both of them were pretty much in the same situation, except at the end of the night, Blue Black still had somewhere to lay his head at. Blue Black lived with his oldest sister, Debra, but he hadn't been to school since elementary and he had to find his next meals the same way as Antoine.

Antoine was pacing across the street from the bus station when he saw Blue Black coming up to him.

"Say Toine, I got us a lick."

"Where 'bout," Antoine asked.

"They got this old white lady smoking a cigarette behind the bus station with her purse sitting on the ground. I know she got some money in that bitch."

"She back there now?" Antoine asked.

"Yea, but look; you can't just run back there and take it, because they got a camera sitting right over your head as soon as you go in that part. The camera is not facing your way. It's facing the back door. You gotta stand sideways with your back turned to the edge of the wall. Like this," Blue Black demonstrated how Antoine had to stand. "This way the camera could only see the back of ya head and not cha face. Ask her for a cigarette first, because the purse sitting behind her legs a lil' bit. When she get it and hand it to you, then you snatch it."

"Aiight," Antoine replied. It never donned on Antoine why the hell Blue Black ain't do it his self.

When Antoine approached the old lady, he seen that he really didn't have to ask for the cigarette, because the purse wasn't under her leg; it was on the side of it. He went ahead and asked anyway and made sure that he was standing the way that Blue Black had told him. After the old lady gave him the cigarette, he asked for a light. Antoine put the cigarette in his mouth and she gave him a light off of the cigarette that she was smoking. When the tip of Antoine's cigarette touched hers, he couldn't help but notice how badly the woman's hand was shaking. That's when Antoine's senses kicked in.

"Thank you, mam." Antoine said, then turned around and walked away.

......................................................................................

"Hello."

"Thank God you picked up," Angela said. "I'm sorry to be calling you so late, but is Antoine over there?"

"Nah uh," I said, then looked at the clock on the dresser and seen that it was 2:47 am. "Angie I haven't seen Antoine since the day he left."

"Monique, please tell me you know where he's at." By the sound of my sister's voice, I could easily tell that she haven't been to sleep in God knows how long.

"He prolly at the Greyhound Bus Station," I said, knowing that he had to be somewhere around there.

"Monique, I need a favor from you." Angela continued, "I need you to see if you could get Lester to go get Antoine from over there and let him stay at your place for tonight.  The pastor will be there tomorrow to pick him up."

"Alright," I said.

Angela didn't know anything about Lester was locked up. Since she got married to the pastor, she hardly comes around the family anymore.  If it wouldn't for Lester being here when she brought those groceries over for Antoine, she wouldn't even know who Lester was.

"Thank you so much lil' sister," Angela replied.  "Call me and let me know when y'all got him."

"Alright Angie."

I hung up with her and looked over at Jon-Jon laying beside me.  I pushed him a couple of times to wake him up.  He complained for a few minutes about going to the Greyhound Bus Station at this time of morning, but he still got his ass up and went.


Jon-Jon walked in the bus station and quickly spotted Andy sitting in the back talking to some Chinese looking dude. Jon-Jon knew Antoine and Andy ran together because he remembered seeing them with each other at Club Vibe's that night.  He started heading in Andy's direction, but after a few steps, he looked to his left and saw Antoine in the refreshment room playing one of the arcade games.

Jon-Jon tapped on the window to get Antoine's attention. After Antoine turned around and seen that it was Jon-Jon calling him, he quickly left the Pac Man game and went holla'd at him.

"Monique told me to come get chu and bring you over there," Jon-Jon said.

"Aiight. Let me go tell my dog I'm out." Antoine said, and went over by Andy.

Antoine related the message to Andy then Andy looked toward the front and seen Jon-Jon standing outside. "Be cool Toine," Andy said, and gave Antoine some dap.

Antoine didn't worry about finding Blue Black to tell him that he was out. He was just glad that somebody came and got him.

Jon-Jon could of drove his Delta 88 but, being that the bus station was only two blocks away, he chose to walk instead. When they got on Convention Street, he told Antoine that his momma had just called worried sick about him. They walked the rest of the way in silence.

When they made it here, Jon-Jon went straight in the room to finish sleeping. I was sitting in the living room smoking a cigarette. Antoine didn't see me because I didn't bother to cut on any lights. He started walking toward the kids' room when I called his name and told him to come here. They had some light coming in through the balcony window, so after Antoine located where my voice came from and realized that I was sitting on the couch, he came and sat on the couch across from me.

"Antoine, you can't continue to do this," were my first words to him.

"I know," Antoine replied.

"Your momma called and said the pastor gon' come pick you up tomorrow."

Antoine didn't respond so I continued. "Antoine, you know that my house is always open to you, huh?"

"Alright," he replied.

"If you ever need to come back for whatever reasons, you're welcome."

"Alright, Monique."

"Alright, you can go in there and get some rest."


LATER THAT DAY AT 7:26 pm:

"Monique, ain't no telling when the last time that boy been to sleep." Tonya said, "'cause this ain't normal."

"Girl, you sho' your nephew ain't dead in there, huh?" Crystal asked.

"He alright, I sent J.J in there to check on him earlier. He's just tired." I said then reached over and answered the ringing phone. "Hello."

"Monique, the pastor outside," Angela said.

"He's out there now?" I asked then went over to the balcony window.

"Yea," Angela replied. "He just called me and told me to

~ 88 ~

tell you."

"I see him Angie.  I'm 'bout to go wake up Antoine now."

"Ok lil' sis," Angela said, then hung up.

After I opened the bedroom door to where Antoine was, I called his name loud enough so he could hear me, but not too loud where I'll scare him.  "Antoine, the pastor out there for you," I told him after he raised his head.

"Alright," Antoine said, wiping his eyes.

# -CHAPTER 7-

(Antoine)

After I got in Pastor Franklin's Lincoln and closed the door behind me, I spoke to him. He had his Kirk Franklin CD playing low, but after a couple of moments, he turned it down completely. He started with, "Your momma told me you was ready to come home."

"Yes sir," I replied.

After letting a couple of seconds pass, he said, "Antoine you know I don't allow back talking in my house. You bet not let it happen again. Do you understand me?"

"Yes sir."

"Alright. As long as we clear on that, you could come home." Pastor Franklin told me then said, "You can go."

"Yes sir," I told him, then opened the door. He started backing out the parking spot as I made my way into the building. I got inside and went in the room to pack my clothes. Not too long after, Monique came in and asked me if I knew that the pastor had left.

"Yea I know he left." I answered.

"What he said?" Monique asked.

"He said I could come back."

"Oh and I guess you supposed to get back the best way you can, huh?"

"I'ma go jump on the city bus." I replied.

Monique left out. About time I finished packing she came back in and told me that my oldest cousin Charles, a.k.a. Big Luck, was on his way to come get me. Just like Coon, Monique, and my grandma, Big Luck didn't live too far from here either. Shit, damn near my whole family lived in the south. We were the only ones that lived all the way across town. Not even fifteen minutes passed when Big Luck walked into the room. "What's up cuz," He said.

I stood up from the bed then said, "What's up gansta," and extended my fist to him. After the daps, I picked up my two sacks and wrapped them around my shoulders.

Me and Big Luck walked out the room then Monique called me. I walked over to her and she asked me if I remembered what we talked about last night. "If you're having any kind of problems at your momma's house with the pastor or anything at all, don't hesitate to come back over here."

"Alright Monique," I told her, feeling good to know that my auntie had my back.

"Give me a hug and you be good." Monique said.

After I gave my favorite auntie a hug, me and Big Luck left. Big Luck had a brown Old School Park Avenue. It wasn't hooked up or anything, but he had a nice Pioneer CD Player in it. We got in and he hands me a blunt with a lighter then turned up the music. As he drove, he put a crack in the window so I wouldn't go there smelling like a pound.

# 18 Months Later

-Chapter 8-

(Monique)

"Happy Birthday to you, Happy Birthday to you, Happy Birthday to Precious, Happy Birthday to you,"

Well, I had a lil' girl and I decided to let Lester name her. He named her Precious because after he got finished with doing the three months in Mississippi...

Oh, I'm sorry. I forgot to tell you that he didn't beat the pistol charge that he picked up in Mississippi, but when he went to court for motion, (motion is when the D.A present all the evidence and any witnesses they have) they dropped the possession of a fire arm down to simple possession and placed him on 2 years of unsupervised probation.

To me, unsupervised probation is their way of saying, "I only want the money from you this time nigger, but if you fuck up again then you gon' pay me both ways. Through doing the time, and when you get out you gon' pay me in cash every month for as long as I say." When Lester came home, he had an eighty-six dollar monthly fine that he had to pay to the state of Mississippi for the next two years.  Plus, he was still on probation here and he had to pay them fifty-three dollars for the year he had remaining with them.  Money hungry bitches!

Lester was shipped to the East Baton Rouge Parish Prison only to be told that he was violated and had a year to do in East Carroll Detention Center.  His two boys, Carl and Troy, after they went to court in Mississippi, they came home the next day.

Back to what I was saying:  Lester named her Precious simply because, after we found out what I was having, every time I had my sister to take me to go see him, all he ever talked about was his precious girl this and his precious girl that.  I guess the name Precious just came naturally.

I also gotta tell you that I moved from out the projects.  The Landlord Ms. Homes kept trying to go up on my Section 8 rent.  Then, she never wanted to fix shit around there.  I remember this one time when everybody in my building hot water heater went off.  It was in the middle of January and it took her two weeks before she had somebody to come out and fix it.

I found a three bedroom house two streets over from the projects.  The house has a nice size backyard, so the kids still have somewhere to play at, and it's fenced in.  When I called the number on the for rent sign, the owner told me that he wanted three-hundred and twenty-five dollars a month and all utilities included except for the light bill.  I knew the light bill wouldn't come up to any more than a hundred and fifteen dollars a month.

When I was younger, my momma was able to scam the Welfare office by getting them to believe I had a mental problem.  Me personally, I don't think anything is mentally wrong with me, even though I have been known throughout the projects to fuck a bitch up at the drop of a dime. Being that my daddy had a history of mental illnesses though, they automatically assumed that it passed down to me. I've been getting six-hundred and seventy-five dollars every month from them since I was thirteen years old. Because of Welfare and the eight-hundred dollars in food stamps I get every month, I never had to work a day in my life.

After Lester called and I talked it over with him, he told me to go ahead and do it, and that his precious little girl needed her own room anyway. I called a few of my nephews over and told'em that I needed them to move my furniture for me. A week later, which was only a few months before Lester came home, I had everything laid out for my man. And even though he had too many clothes as it was, I still went out and bought him a few more outfits with a brand new pair of Air Force 1's.

Me and Crystal is still close. She comes to the house whenever she could, but we haven't been out in a good lil' minute. Either, Kevin and her kids got her tied up or Lester and Precious got my hands full. We knew our partying days would come to an end as soon as the baby came anyway.

My girl Tonya ended up moving back with her momma. She said she was missing her kids too much and that she ain't wanna take them away from their grandparents because her momma and daddy have had them practically since they were born. I think it's a good thang that she decided to move back home. Tonya had gotten entirely too wild out chea. She had a different nigga at her place damn near every night. Hopefully through her being back at her momma's house and seeing those three pretty lil' girls of hers that she calm down.

I had told Lester that it was crazy to throw a birthday party for a one year old child; it's not like they knew what was going on anyway, but he insisted on doing something and that he was only gonna invite a few friends over.

The party was nice. Everybody bought Precious some clothes, shoes, or either a new toy. I did a light decorating here in the living room and bought her another outfit too. Everything was whining down now. All the kids were in the room playing the game, Lester and his boys were in the backyard, and I had Precious in my arm while I was sitting on the couch talking to Crystal.

"Girl, you know Lester talking about taking me to get my driver's license, huh?"

"Damn Monique, you said that like it's a bad thing." Crystal said.

"It is," I told her. "Girl, I don't want no car. I'm 26 years old and if I ain't had one in all this time then I don't need one."

"Well, you the first person I ever heard say that. I wish Kevin would tell me that if I got my driver's license then he'll buy me a car. I'd be at the D.M.V 6:00 in the morning with a pencil behind my ear like, 'bitch where the test at?'"

"Momma," Jonathan yelled out from the room. "J.J snatched the draw stick out my hand!"

"J.J!" I yelled.

"Mom that boy lying." J.J said while coming in the living room. "Ain't nobody snatched no draw stick from him. He just trying to get somebody in trouble."

"J.J, I know y'all better stop all that bullshit in there and take turns before I take that game away from y'all." I said.

"Yes mam," J.J mumbled and went back in the room.

"Doria and Micheal," Crystal yelled out. After they came, she asked, "Y'all being good in there, huh?"

"Yes mam." Both of'em responded.

"What y'all sister in there doing?" Crystal asked, referring to her youngest daughter Jasmine.

"She sitting down playing with them toys." Doria answered.

"Ok, y'all could go back in there."

-CHAPTER 9-

=The Plot=

"Troy, tell me about that brod again." Lester asked.

"Damn Lester, I been telling you for the past two days now. Clean out cha fucking ears." Troy said. "Look, the bitch said the nigga throw a dice game every night. Nothin' but big balling ass niggas be in there rocking platinum chains, Rolex's, and fifty-thousand dollars pinky rings and shit. It be 'bout fifteen niggas and each one of'em have at least seventy-five grand on'em."

"Mane, how you know fa'sho you got the brod and that she ain't just playing games wit' chu?" Carl asked. The group of three stood in a small circle in Monique's back yard on a sunny day as the plot began.

"Nigga I got the bitch right chea," Troy said, while raising his right arm to pat his self on the side. Meaning he had her under his wing. "The bitch ain't playing games 'cause she knows that I'll blow her fucking head off. Plus, she had me to come over there last night to check out everything. Nigga, I rode pass that house and saw nothin' but BMWs, Benz's, and Navigators parked all in the grass and shit.

Mane bruh I'm telling you, all the bitch fuck with is hard core gangsta ass niggas. She said she been wantin' to leave his ass alone ever since he let his cousin disrespect her and call her all kinds of bitches and hoes while he just stood there with his mouth closed. Only reason she stayed with him after that is because the nigga caked up; she wanna get some of that bread out his ass first."

"So what, she want us to kick in the doe while everybody in there shooting dice?" Lester asked.

"Nah uh," Troy answered. "She said when we get there, the back window to the guest room gon' already be broke and left opened for us. All we gotta do is climb through it, lay niggas down, get it and bounce. Its gon' be somebody in there feeling like they're moe powerful than a bullet and moe faster than a trigger finger that's itching so when we prov'em wrong its gon' be in silence." Troy raised his shirt and pulled out a seventeen shot 9 mm Beretta with a silencer on the end of it. "I got three of these and two glocks."

"Mane, what the fuck," Lester asked, while looking back and forward from Carl to Troy. "Carl, what the fuck happen to Troy? This ain't that same nigga that I left out chea. I leave for 15 months, come home and this nigga on some real live gangsta shit." Lester began to smile. "Yeeeaaa, this what the fuck I'm talkin' about." He then slapped hands with Troy. "Where you get that bitch from?"

"When the gun and knife show came a couple months ago, I paid my sister to get me a rack of shit." Troy answered. "Nigga I got a bullet proof vest and all at the crib. She already reported the shit in as stolen so everything good."

"Carl, this nigga got everything mapped out." Lester said.

"Yea, he did his homework, and the shit sound like it could work." Carl spoke.

"It's gon' work," Troy stated.

"Alright, but look, we gon' need two moe niggas with us." Lester said. "At least four people gotta go in the house."

"Man, that's five mouths." Troy complained.

"Five mouths," Lester said, while looking at Troy like he shitted on his self; "Nigga you tripping on how many people eating? You must be trying to get cha crazy ass killed and take me and Carl to the grave wit' chu huh? You said it's gon' be 'bout fifteen niggas in there with around seventy-five grand on'em, then we taking jewelry and all. It's prolly a million dollars in diamonds in there alone. Over two million dollars we trying to come up on and you wanna trip on it being five niggas!"

"Aiight aiight," Troy said, while flagging his hand for Lester to calm down. "So it's on?"

"Carl, you down?" Lester asked.

"Shit, this too good of an opportunity for me not to be; fucking right I'm in." Carl answered.

"Alright," Lester said. "I'ma get the other two niggas for the job. "Troy, you got five guns so keep two of'em for yourself. Carl, what happened to that .38 special you left at the house that day we went to Mississippi?"

"I still got it," Carl answered. "I don't have a silencer on it though."

"That's cool. You the driver so hopefully you won't need it anyway." Lester said, then turned his attention back to Troy. "I'ma take one of those nines you got and give the two glocks to the niggas I bring. Call ya girl and see what's a good time for us to come."

"Can't do that," Troy said. "I stopped calling her as soon as I seen she was serious about it. I don't want the nigga to think she's messing around on him. I want him to continue calling her his adorable little princess." Troy let out a slight chuckle, "Bitch gon' call me later on."

"Damn Troy, chill out with all these bitches." Carl said. "What's her name?"

"Oh yea," Troy said, and laughed again. "Her name is Shanice."

"So what Shanice want out the deal?" Lester asked, then continued with. "All she want is for you to be her man; move to Miami with her and start a family?"

"Yea, that's one of the things, but she want a hundred grand too." Troy answered.

"Troy how long have you been messing with this chic?" Carl asked.

"I been knowing her for 'bout three years now. Back when I use to mess with her girl Crystal. I knew she was digging me then, but she was messing with some crazy ass nigga that had her ass on straight lockdown. Crystal use to tell me all about how the nigga was putting his foot up Shanice's ass every time she stepped out of line." Troy continued. "After all this time, I finally caught up with her in Cortana Mall last weekend. When she laid eyes me and realized who I was, nigga she damn near ran out of

Journeys to give me a hug. After I met up with her at Motel 6 that night and fucked the shit out her, she started telling me all kinds of stuff about the nigga."

"Aiight then," Lester said, and looked at Carl. "It's on. Troy, go ahead and tell her to cut the green light on for us. We gon' give her the hundred grand she wants, but if we start blasting in there, we might-as-well knock her ass off with everybody else. She knows too much. Where the house at anyway?"

"It's in Scotlandvile," Troy answered.

"Let's go roll by there." Lester said. "I wanna check it out."

"Let's go." Troy replied.

Lester, Carl, and Troy started walking toward the back door of the house. When they got inside and in the living room, Lester went sat on the couch beside Monique. Troy went got Precious from out of Crystal's arms and held her in the air while him and Carl made her laugh by making funny faces. Lester told Monique that he was leaving and asked if she needed anything from the store while he was out. She told him that she was ok so Lester gave her a kiss then went over and got Precious from Troy and gave her a kiss too before he hand her to Monique. The three then they left the house.

All three of them had a ride, but they chose to go in Troy's Cutlass Supreme because his was the only one that had tented windows. It was also sitting on some seventeen inch Bravo's with two twelves in the trunk. Lester and Carl's wouldn't as decorated as Troy's.

Lester had a 1984 Camaro I-rock. The car wasn't in bad shape or anything. Matter of fact, it looked damn good with the platinum paint job and the original Camaro rims, which was in the same condition as when he first bought the car from a guy name Bo seven years ago. Lester was sixteen back then and the only thing that he ever did to it was put in a Clarion CD player. He been wanting to do more, but every time he got the money for the bigger rims or the two TV's that he planned to put in the sun visor, the money always went on his drug habit and clothes shopping fetish or either he'll lose it in a dice game.

Lester stood at 6.2, dark skinned, with 6 gold teeth at the bottom of his mouth, and rocked a low hair cut. What attracted Monique to him was not only because of his looks, but because of the way that he conducted his self around her. Even though Lester liked sprinkling angel dust in his blunts, Monique never found out about it because he hid it so well from her and her kids. He never brought it anywhere near the house and whenever he was away and he did it, he always waited a couple of hours for his high to go down before he went back around them.

Carl had just gotten his car three months ago from Steve's Car Lot over on Jefferson Highway. After he lost his Nissan to the cop that chose to take the law in his own hand by shooting out Carl's tire, he had to go a whole nine months with putting up with his momma's mouth every time he asked to borrow her car. Carl's looks favored the looks of the old school rapper Mac 10's, except Carl wasn't as light skinned as Mac 10. Carl was 5.7, light brown, low hair cut, and little bit on the chubby side.

Troy could of took the interstate and been there in less than fifteen minutes, but he wanted to kill some time by driving through all the different hoods that was in between the South Side and Scotlandvile. He drove through Easy town, Fairfield,

Park Town, North Dale, and CC Lock down.

About time they made it there, it was just turning dark. When Troy stopped at the stop sign that was up the street from the house, he turned down his music.

"That's the house there," Troy said, "the brown one with the green STS in front of it."

"Aiight, we see it." Lester said, as him and Carl zoom their eyes in the same direction as Troy's.

Troy began driving toward the house going slow enough so that they could get a good look at it, but not too slow where they'll look suspicious to any of the neighbors that just so happen to be looking out their windows.

"That's Shanice car." Troy said, looking at the Cadillac. "She said the nigga drive a black one just like it."

"How many bedrooms is it?" Lester asked, paying attention to the windows on both sides of the house.

"Prolly three," Troy answered. "They don't have any kids living there. It's just them two." Troy came up with the number three by the guest room Shanice told him about, their room, and he figured that by the size of the house that it might've had one more.

"Make the block," Lester told him.

As they passed the house, Troy looked back at one of the back windows and noticed a light on. He thought about calling Shanice but then he thought, "She could be gone with him and they just left a light on to make a potential jacker, us, think that somebody was home." Either way, he didn't want to chance it.

While they were coming up the back street, Lester told Troy to stop. "That's the house there." Lester said, looking in between two houses and seeing Shanice's. "You know which window is for the guest room?"

"Nah uh," Troy answered. "She just told me that it was one of the back one's." Troy's Nextel started ringing. "This her here," Troy said, looking at the number that displayed on the screen. "Where you at," He quickly asked, after he flipped open the phone.

"Well damn, hey to you too, my man." Shanice said.

"Fa'real ma, where you at," Troy repeated.

"I'm at my house," Shanice answered. "Why?"

"Because I'm behind it," Troy told her. "Look out cha back window."

Shanice hurried and went to the guest room. "I see you baby." She said, looking out the blinds. "Can you see me?" Shanice went over and turned on the light.

"Yea I see you," Troy answered. "Is that the guest room?"

"Yea this it," Shanice answered.

"Aiight ma," Troy said, and slowly drove off. "So when is a good time?"

"What today is; Tuesday?" Shanice said. "Well, y'all could do it tomorrow night, but on Fridays is when the most nigga's be here. Shit, we cut no less than thirty-five grand on Fridays alone."

Troy put the Nextel on speaker phone. "How much you said y'all cut?"

"We cut fifteen to twenty grand every night, but on Fridays the house takes in around thirty-five to forty." Shanice said.

"Shit, we need to be robbing him then." Lester said, loud enough for Shanice to hear. "Where that nigga keep his safe?"

"Your guess will be as good as mine. He might be pussy, but he ain't stupid." Shanice said. "He doesn't keep any money at the house but chump change. After every game, he takes all the money he made for that day and drive out to some secret location."

"Damn, you don't know where?" Troy asked.

"Well if I knew, it wouldn't be a secret. Now would it." Shanice asked.

Lester grabbed the phone from Troy. "Let me see it," He said, and put the phone close to his mouth so she could hear him without him yelling. "Describe the guest room to me. Matter of fact, what the whole house look like in there? Where the other bedrooms at, the bathrooms, the dining room; tell me everything about it."

Shanice described the whole house to him, leaving out nothing. Then Lester asked, "Who live in those two houses that we were looking between?"

"An old lady stay in the one directly behind mines, and some dude and his girl just moved in the other one." Shanice told him.

"Aiight, you could go ahead and set up everything for this Friday," Lester said. "What's a good time?"

"The best time will be like at 3:00. By then, everybody be dun close down shop and came over here to make some extra ends. Come any time between three and three thirty."

Lester hand the phone back to Troy.

Shanice's boyfriend having money but living in that lil' small ass house didn't surprise them at all. A lot of hustlers from the hood that had big money never left the hood because they were afraid of attracting unwanted eyes, (F.B.I.).

"Say ma, call me back in an hour." Troy said into the speaker.

"Hold up a minute." Shanice quickly said. "Y'all got me huh?"

"Yea you know we got chu ma," Troy reassured her.

"Will I see you tonight?" Shanice asked.

"When you call me back," Troy answered.

"Aiight," Shanice said, and hung up.

While Troy was getting off the phone with Shanice, Lester was calculating the numbers in his head. He figured them hitting for a million dollars in cash. If so, then that would mean that everybody get two hundred grand a piece. Being that Troy found the lic, he was entitled to keep his whole half. Lester was gonna take twenty-five thousand out of his cut, Carl's, and the two people he bring to pay Shanice her one hundred thousand.

"Who you got in mind," Carl asked.

"Well I know Lil' Tim gon' be one." Lester answered.

"Aiight, Lil' Tim's silent," Troy said. "Who else?"

"I'm thinking 'bout bringing Joe," Lester told'em.

"Nah uh man, I know you ain't talking 'bout your playful ass cousin Joe." Troy said, thinking back on all the times when they were younger and Joe used to drive him about his payless tennis shoes that his momma made him wear. "I ain't never seen that bitch serious before."

"Nah man that nigga ain't with all the bullshit no moe," Lester said. "Then if it's about money, that nigga shape up quick, fast, and in a hurry."

Troy pulled into a gas station on Plank Road and all three of them got out and went in the store. They each got a beer, but Lester and Troy got a pack of cigarettes also. Carl didn't smoke cigarettes. He went ahead and got three cigars for the half ounce that Lester had. Troy put fifteen on pump three then one by one they walked out of the store.

While Troy pumped, Carl sat behind the wheel with the door opened and his left foot on the ground as he rolled up. You would think that by it being the month of February that it would be cold outside. Tonight felt damn good though. Lester lend against the back of the car in a white tee shirt, some blue jeans Eko pants, and a brand new pair Jordan's as he enjoyed the night air. He couldn't help but think of how good it felt to be home.

While Lester was incarcerated, he did a lot of things that he now regrets. Lester's jose consisted of gambling, beating niggas up for the hell of it, and doing just about anything to past the time. Whenever he got his hands on some ecstasy, the next day he would find himself throwing up in the toilet from images of the night before.

When Lester was younger, he had a bad case of ADHD. Attention Deficiency Hyperactive Disorder. As he got older, he learned how to keep it under control some, but there were still those times when he completely lost it. In jail, he had absolutely no control over it. The disorder would take over him so bad that there were times when he used to wonder if he would make it out. Especially, when he beat up one of the guards in the chow house and got rebooked. Rebook is when you do something in jail, like stab somebody or beat somebody up a little too bad, and the officers take you up to central booking and give you a street charge for it. They finger print you again, take your picture again; they do the whole nine yards. Because Lester broke the guard's jar, they charged him with second degree battery on a correction officer.

When he went to court for it, they gave him two years jail time. He came out good because they ran it concurrent with the year he was already doing.

In the state jails, the only way they made you do eighty-five percent of your time is when you've been convicted of a crime that's considered as a capital offense, meaning a murder charge, arm robbery, or rape. Lester only had to do half of the two years, which meant, Lester's out date never changed. That's something that he never told Monique about.

All three of their minds were on the money that they were finna come up on and how they planned to spend it. While Troy was pumping the gas and watching the cars passing up and down Plank Road, still in a zone, a red Dodge Neon pulled up to the pump next to his. Lester and Troy's eyes immediately locked in on it.

Three girls got out. The one that got out the back stood at five nine, wearing a blue tee shirt with some blue jeans pants that hugged every inch of her ass and thighs. The second one, passenger seat, was a little shorter than the first girl, wearing blue jeans with a white shirt and a brown zip up hood over it. The driver was the shortest out the group, standing at five four, wearing khaki pants with a red shirt. All of them wore their hair down their backs, and all of them had big asses.

"I meeeaaan that; look what we dun ran across!" Troy said, rubbing his hands together and looking at the driver. "It's on!"

Troy started walking to the driver as all three of them turned around and began looking at him crazy. I don't know what the driver was putting on that front for because she was already scoping Troy out way before he seen her, or should I say she was scoping out his car, which is the reason she pulled up to the pump next to his in the first place. Even though she had already chosen Troy's car, when she saw him, she saw that he wouldn't ugly at all.

Troy stood at five ten, light skinned, with some long brads in his head. Troy always had gotten the attention from the ladies. Even when he wore his Jordan's with only the word Jordan spelled out on the shoe and not the Jordan sign. Females always did acknowledge him, but back then, they wouldn't give him the satisfaction of telling people that they went together. They would only conversed with him on the phone and some would even go as far as letting him fuck just to see what he was packing.

Lester finished pumping the last of the gas that Troy walked off from and forgot all about. Then he and Carl walked over to the other two girls.

"What up wit' ch'all ma," Troy asked the driver.

"Nothin', finna go to work," She answered.

Troy dem already knew that girls as fine as they were, working at night, could only mean one thing.

"What club y'all working at," Lester asked the girl he was standing in front of.

"Over at Magic City." She answered.

"Let us go pay for this gas right quick," The driver said. "We coming back."

After the girls walked off, Lester, Carl, and Troy got into a semi huddle.

"These bitches fine," Lester said. "But I don't pay for pussy."

"Me neither, but there's always an exception," Troy said.

"Mane bruh fuck these hoes. We need to be focusing on this money." Carl said.

"Yea you right," Lester agreed. "Friday is three days away, and me and you Carl gotta find out what car we gon' use. Troy, you stay focused on Shanice's ass; we don't need any last minute fuck ups. Let's just get these brods number and get back at them on the weekend."

"That's what's up," Troy said.

# -CHAPTER 10-

Everyone met up at the Holiday Inn at two o'clock that morning to go over all the details. Lester and Carl had just returned to the room from getting what took the two of them forty-five minutes to find; which is a four door Dodge Ram Truck. They almost gave up and settled for a Dodge Durango instead, but the Durango didn't have a Hemi under the hood. Being that the police station was only a block away from Shanice's house, Lester knew they would need something that could have them off that side of town as quick as possible. A Hemi was perfect for the job. They found the truck in a white neighborhood on side of the road parked in front of someone's house.

Carl is what you would call an expert at stealing cars. He started when he was eleven years old. Back then, he would steal a car almost every night to go joy riding in. The night of his fourteenth birthday was his first time ever being chased by a cop, but by then, the rookie was no match for Carl's driving skills. After only a few quick turns, Carl put the pedal to the floor and quickly gained three blocks ahead of the cop. The rest was history.

Lester was sitting on the bed loading the sixty-round clip to the Mac 11.

"Say Lester, I don't think you should bring that bitch." Troy said. "We don't plan on letting them niggas get any shots off."

"Fa'real man, you let that bitch go and y'all gon' be busting at the cops and all. Because they for damn sho' gon' be waiting in front of that house with their guns out ready to blast at whoever run out there with a gun in his hand." Said Carl.

"Hopefully I won't need it, but just in case shit gets crazy, we killing everythang." Lester said.

"It's not," Troy disagreed, then went in his pockets and pulled out a hand full of Zip Ties. "Take some of these." He gave Lil' Tim half. "We tying them niggas the fuck up."

"Fucking right," Lil' Tim said, as he took another hit from the blunt. "Now we ain't gotta worry 'bout watching our backs while we go in them niggas' pockets.

"Give us the time we need to get back too," Joe added.

As soon as Troy phone started ringing, he answered it on speaker, "Yea."

"It's thirteen niggas, only two of'em strapped that I know of." Shanice was whispering. "The light skin nigga wearing the red, black, and blue stripe Polo shirt; you'll know exactly who I'm talking 'bout when you see him 'cause he's the shortest one in the room. He got a gun. And another tall dark skinned nigga with a blue bandana tied around his head got one too. I could see his pocking out his shirt."

"Aiight ma; we on our way now," Troy told her.

"Ok," Shanice whispered, then hung up her cell phone, flushed the toilet, and went back in the living room.

"Green light," Troy said.

Lester stood up from the bed then cocked the Mac 11. "Let's ride."


The temperature had dropped since the other night at the gas station. It was back to normal February weather. Louisiana weather could be crazy at times. They all left the room wearing black jeans with a black hood. Lester and Troy had on black leather jackets. After they all got in the truck, Lester reiterated the plan to make sure everyone was on point, but really he was directing it at Lil' Tim. The group been knowing each other for a long time now because they were all from the same hood, but this was Lester, Carl, and Troy's first time ever pulling a 211 with Lil' Tim and Joe.

Over the years, Lester had been hearing a lot of stuff throughout the south about the work Lil' Tim been putting in. That's why Lil' Tim's name was at the top of Lester's list. Lester knew he wouldn't hesitate to pull the trigger. His only problem with Lil' Tim was that Lil' Tim chose to get high before hittin' a lick. Lester heard of people preforming better when they were under the influence, but he had just never seen anyone who did. Plus, he knew the way that drugs made him act. Some of the stupid things he did when he was high he don't even like to think about.  Lester ain't wanna see a two million dollar deal get messed up over a simple mistake.  Lester chose his cousin Joe strictly because he knew Joe was 'bout getting money.  Joe was a street nigga, so afterwards Lester knew he wouldn't run his mouth like a brod.

When they came to the stop sign that was up the street from the house, they looked at all of the cars sitting in front of the house.

"Let's get out here," Lester said.

"You niggas be careful in that bitch." Carl said, as the rest started opening doors.  He then drove off in the direction of the house.

As they started walking, Lester looked at the Wal-Mart watch on his wrist.  He pushed the bottom to make the light come on and saw that it was 3:23 am.  The street was dead; nobody outside, and no lights on in any of the houses they passed.  When they came to the two houses that were behind Shanice's, each dug in their pockets and pulled out a black mass and a pair black gloves.

They secured their face and hands then quickly ran between the two houses and jumped the gate without making any noticeable noises.  They came to the window and seen that everything was exactly like Shanice said it would be.  Broke and left opened.  Shanice must have just left the room and decided on moving the blinds out of their way as well because they were pulled all the way up.

The light was off in the room, but after they climb

through, they were able to make everything out by the street light coming through the window. They crept silently to the door. Besides from the loud music on the other side, they also heard the sound of a toilet being flushed.

Lester thought about opening the door and putting a hot slug in who ever came out of the bathroom. He didn't because he ain't want to take a chance in the nigga falling and making any noises that would alert the rest. They stayed in the room. When they heard the bathroom door open and close, then the sound of footsteps come out and drift down the hallway, Lester opened the door to peek his head out.

One behind the other, they left the room and put their backs against the wall and guns pointing to the end of the short hallway. Troy and Joe was on one side, while Lester and Lil' Tim were on the other. The four wasn't walking fast, but they weren't moving slow either. They walked at a paste that would have them off of the hall before someone came and ruined their surprise. When they came to the bedroom that Shanice told them about, they seen that the light was left on and the door was open. The room was on Troy's side of the hall. Lester, Lil Tim, and Joe kept their eyes on the living room as Troy looked in the bedroom and seen that no one was in there.

They continued to walk toward the light and the music. The closer they got, the clearer they heard the sounds of deep voices and dice clicking. Shanice told them that the living room has two sides to it and that both sides contained a pool table for the dice shooters. Back at the room when Troy was on the phone with Shanice, she told them that there were thirteen people. Since then, two more niggas from out of Baker came. There were seven shooters on one side of the living room and eight on the other.   The group of four was about to stand in the middle of fifteen hustlers, knowing that every one of them could very well be strapped.

The kitchen was on Lester's side of the hall, when Lester came to it, he looked into the right side of the living room and saw someone that was no more than four feet ten inches wearing a black, blue, and red stripe Polo shirt.  The little but grown man was standing beside three dudes.  All of their backs were turned to Lester as they watched the dice man roll the dice.  Lester signaled with his head and told Troy to go ahead.  Troy knelt down low then quickly dipped into the kitchen.

Lester, Lil' Tim, and Joe stormed the living room.

"Nobody fucking move!"  Lester screamed, then quickly shot someone three times in the chest as soon as he attempted to pull a gun from out of his pants that his fingers barley got the chance to touch.  The person that Lester shot was the guy with the blue bandana around his head that Shanice told them about.

Lil' Tim was about to shoot the midget in the Polo shirt on G.P. until he saw just how scared the nigga looked.  "Don't fucking move!"  Lil' Tim spoke, as all three of'em waved their guns around the room.

As Troy came to the other side of the kitchen, he noticed a sawed off twelve gage shot gun leaning against the wall.  Troy then looked into the living room and saw a fat man a few feet away from the wall, steady inching his way back.  He heard Lester screaming out to everyone not to move, but fat boy thought he was just the slickest.  The fat man got all the way to the wall then reached his arm back.

"This what the fuck you looking foe fat boy?" Troy asked as he pointed the double barrel at the back of the fat man's head. "I oughta blow ya fucking head off, bitch. Lay on the fucking floe." The fat man quickly got down on his stomach.

"Everybody lay the fuck down," Troy screamed, cocking the gage as he entered the living room.

Some quickly got down and others chose to take their time.

"What the hell you and that bitch still standing foe," Lester asked, looking at a tall guy with a low hair cut standing next to Shanice, who was the only female in the room.

"How the fuck y'all gon' come into my shit and try to rob me?" Shanice's boyfriend asked.

Lester answered by simply giving him a slug with the Nine Miller Meter. Shanice's boyfriend fell to the floor clutching the bottom of his stomach where Lester shot him.

After everyone realized how quick and easy it was for Lester to murder someone, they cooperated a little quicker. The group gained complete control of the house. Troy and Lil' Tim went around with the zip ties.

"Bitch ass niggas robbing us, y'all niggas dead." Somebody that was wearing about ten chains around his neck raised his head, looked around, then continued. "Don't think this the end of it."

Lil' Tim went stood over him and pointed the glock

between his eyes. "Shut up and turn around," Lil Tim didn't yell nor was he aggressive when he said it, but the way he said it, was more threatening than anything.

"Fuck you! I ain't turning around shit. If y'all gon' kill me, you gon' look me in my eyes when you do it. You not about to shoot me behind my fucking head," Brave soul.

"That's cool too," Lil' Tim said, looking him straight in the eyes with his finger on the trigger.

"Trouble turn ya crazy ass around!" Someone quickly spoke out. "Nigga don't die over this shit. We can make it back in two weeks."

Trouble continued complaining to his self while at the same time listening to his friend by turning around. Lil' Tim tied up Trouble's hands and feet.

After Troy and Lil' Tim had everyone tied, Lester pulled out a white pillow case from his inside jacket pocket and went around grabbing money off of both pool tables. Troy went around with another pillow case and took all the jewelry off everyone's necks, wrists, fingers, and even ears. Lil' Tim and Joe each had a roll of duct tape that they went around putting on everyone's mouth. They emptied their pockets and ripped them of every stone they wore.

Lester opened the front door then stood outside and looked toward the end of the street. Moments later, Carl came with the truck, stopping it in the middle of the street in front of the house.

Lester went back inside the house and let the rest of the

crew walk out first. As Lester was the last to leave, he turned off the living room light and closed the door behind him. Everybody was in the truck but Lester so Lil' Tim left the back door opened for him, but when he saw Lester go to the back and climbed up, he closed it.

Lester sat down in the back of the truck facing the house. Before Carl pulled off, Lester grabbed the Mac 11 that's been strapped around his back the whole night and aimed it at the house. Then, "Blr, blr, blr, blr, blr, blr, blr, blr, blr, blr, blr, blr, blr, blr, blr, blr, blr, blr, blr, blr, blr, blr, blr, blr, blr."

"Eeeeeeerrrrrrrrrrrrrrrrr."

-CHAPTER 11-

(Antoine)

"How's the congregation doing today? It's always a blessing to be back in the house of the Lord. Amen. Today we're gonna pick up from where we left off, talking about love. Amen. Everybody turn your bible with me to the Book of Corinthians; chapter thirteen. When somebody get it read the first verse for me."

Me and Fred sat in the back with our bibles in our laps. Pastor Franklin has been having church here at the house for the past two weeks now. The church building was getting some remodeling done to it. The pastor didn't have a big congregation. It was only seven families of threes and fours. The townhouse we lived in had four bedrooms. The pastor had my lil' brother move his bed along with everything else in my lil' brother's room into the room with Lashey. Then he simply used the empty room for the temporary sanctuary by putting an Alter and about twenty five fold up chairs in it. Me and Trap had our own room. But my room wasn't necessarily what you would call a room, I slept in the closet. Hold up a minute nah; my closet is big and it's laid out.

And it's not just a closet. It's a closet, a middle room with a long table in it, and a bathroom combined. Next to my momma and the pastor's room, I think I got the best room in the house.

"Verse: 8 say's: 'Love never fails. But whether there are prophecies, they will fail; whether there are tongues, they will cease; whether there is knowledge, it will vanish away.' Can you hear me out there?" Pastor Franklin said. "Somebody read verse nine for me."

Sister Johnson stood up. "For we know in part and we prophesy in part." Sister Johnson paused after she read the verse.

"Continue with verse ten," The pastor told her.

"But when that which is perfect has come, then that which is in part will be done away. Amen." Sister Johnson sat down.

"Hallelujah," The pastor said. "When that which is perfect has come, then that which is in part will be done away. Can anybody hear me out there? It is no in between stuff with God. You want to praise God on Sunday, but be in Club Dreams on Monday. Amen. You want to keep his commandments all year round, but when the holidays come you want to bend them a lil' bit. Amen. You don't wanna get too drunk, but you gon' just have a lil' taste of the Hennessy. Lord, I'ma just have a glass of Gin, but I'm not gon' get drunk though. Can anybody hear me out there?

Now on the other hand; you stay the same way all year

round. You been this way since you was a kid. You don't bother anybody. You feel like you're the most innocent person in the world. You don't drink, you don't smoke none of them trees, you don't go to clubs, you don't listen to rap music; you the world's most innocent person. Y'all don't hear me out there? You the same way all year round; you don't do any kind of evil. But at the same time, you don't do any good either.

You don't go to church, you don't read your bible; you don't praise the Lord or anything. You're in neutral all year round, lukewarm. You're neither hot nor cold. And you really think that you gon' be accepted into the Kingdom of God. Come on now, Mr. and Mrs. Innocent. That ain't gon' work. Either you is or you ain't, you for him or you against him, simple as that. I repeat myself, there's no in between with God. Can I get an Amen?"

When the pastor had his Deacon to close out, and church was over, he took the congregation out to eat. I was in my room working on one of my latest raps. When I heard the door open, I raised my head to look in the big mirror on my wall and noticed Stacy coming in.

After she closed the door behind her, she walked over next to where I was sitting in the chair and she sat up on the table. "What chu doing in here?" She asked.

"Shit," I responded, as I stood up.

I moved my chair out the way, took a step back, then reached my arm toward the wall and turned the nob on it until the light went all the way off. Stacy wore a black dress to church that day. I walked over to her unfastening my pants. She had her legs wide open so I walked straight in between them. I dug my right hand in my back pocket and pulled out one of the condoms that I kept with me on a daily basis. She must've took off her panties downstairs or either she didn't wear any to church that day because after I quickly strapped up I aimed for the hole and pushed straight in.

I put my arms under both of her legs as I lift them higher and started hitting it. I was plugging in her deep and hard, until she wrapped her arms around my neck while biting down on the side of it. The way that she held me so tight it forced me to stop. When she loosened her grip and pulled her teeth from out of my neck, I tried to continue the happy process, but she told me to hold up a minute.

Stacy started pushing at my chest causing me to let go of her legs and come out of her. The pastor's daughter then got down and walked out of the room. That's when I realized. She beat me to the finish line.


Nah hold up a minute, and hear my side of the story. Stacy is four years older than me. And we're not the ones that told my momma and her daddy to get married. The two of us have been having sex now since I was twelve years old. Stacy never before lived with us. She just always used to come spend the night. She lived with her white momma over in Dixie. Her momma is white and her daddy's black, so you could imagine how Stacy looked standing at 5.6, big titties with the Mariah Carey's complexion, Halle Berry's hair style, and weighing 130 pounds.  I also wanna take this time out to say, "Big up's to Stacy! You were my first."

-CHAPTER 12-

(Antoine)

**Ninth grade at McKinley High:** I had finally convinced my momma to let me go to school on this side of town. At first, she refused to let me because I enrolled myself in McKinley Middle last year, had that fight and got put out. But after I started going to Valley Park Alternative School and I pulled my grades up, she told me that if I passed that year then we'll talk about it. At the first sign of trouble though, she'll have me going to Broadmoor High where all the white folks went to school at. My former partner Peter White, who I beat up, didn't go to McKinley High anyway. But even if he did, I already did what I wanted to do so I wouldn't gon' mess with him no more, and I know damn well he wouldn't wanna do anything with me so as far as I was concern, it was over.

On that Battery and Trespassing Charge, I never did go to court for it. My momma never brought it up, so neither did I. I think the reason why she didn't bring it up was because she didn't want a probation officer coming out to the house. Most likely that's all they was gon' do anyway; put me on some lame ass papers telling me to do this, that, and a whole lot of other bullshit that wouldn't gon' never happen.

I was posted up at school that morning, like usual, with my dudes Jonny, B-Roc, and a few other people that I hung with. I noticed another one of my dogs, Lanelle Shepherd, come out of the school's cafeteria drinking one of the milks that they gave out to us in there. As he continued walking, he stopped by the garbage can and threw away the empty milk carton. When he got about ten feet away from us, he slowed his paste. I picked my book sack up from off the ground and went over to meet him. After we slapped and gripped each other's hand, we started walking toward the back of the school. Lanelle Shepherd knew a lot of people in my family so he started asking about my brother and my cousin Peewee; just bullshit questions. Then he reached in his pocket and pulled out a small knot.

He hand me twenty-five dollars so I went in my pocket and gave him a twenty bag and the five dollar bill back.

"This the last of it my nigga," I said. "I'ma be good tomorrow though."

"You getting some moe of this huh," He asked, after putting the merchandise in his pocket "'Cause this shit A-1."

"That's all I fuck with roune." I responded.

We continued kicking it on our way back to the front of the school. The first hour bell started ringing, and that's when I saw her. Walking toward me in some skin tight blue jeans, hips swaying from side to side, ass that you could see from the front, flawless face, long hair. I mean, she was everything a nigga could imagine.

"Hey Toine," She said, before we hugged then gave each other two three second kisses.

"What's up, Boo Bear."


Hope Nicole Davis. No doubt, I had the baddest girl in the school. She was a freshman too, and she never been with anyone around here. But to top it all off, besides the looks and the jazziness, she never really been with a nigga, period. I had me a virgin on my hand. Say, I never had one of those before. She gon' be my first, or should I say, I'ma be her first. I'm talking and laughing at the same time right now but aye, we gon' be each other's first. Real talk.


The only class we took together was seventh hour P.E. Both of our first hour classes were right across the hall from each other.

"Your brother brought you to school this morning?" I asked, as we walked down the crowded hallway.

"Yea, he told me to tell you what's up." Hope answered.

We could barely hear each other from all the noise of the students going to first hour. When we got in front of ours, we hugged again, then she went in her class and I went in mine's.

I walked in the gym for seventh hour and saw one of my dogs from elementary school on the basketball court, hitting jump shot after jump shot from the three point line. Bakari Walker was always a dog in sports. In elementary, he was the fastest on the football team. Well besides from another one of my classmates named, Jarvis Jackson. They used to call Jarvis, Baby Lightning.

Me myself, I never got into any of the sports at school. I wanted to though. When we moved to the bottom on East Harrison Street, my momma transferred me from Dufrocq to Buchanan which was the same school that Bakari went to. I tried out for the football team there and I know for a fact that I would've been one of the coldest. I had that natural quickness with me. After tryout practice, I went home that day and told my momma that I wanted to play, but when she talked it over with the pastor he said I couldn't and that I must've been trying to play football so I could stay after school and mess around with some lil' girl.

"Bakari, I see you still think you the truth huh?" I asked, after I walked over to him.

"You know it!" Bakari said, while hitting his fifth three in a roll, which is every shot that he put up since I came in the gym. "And I prove myself at every game."

The bell ringed so I went sat in one of the chairs where the rest of my classmates were sitting. The chairs were sitting in front of a 26" TV. The TV along with a VCR was sitting on an iron TV stand. When Hope walked in, she came sat in the chair next to me and gave me a quick kiss.

"What time you went to sleep last night?"

"Right after we got off the phone," She answered. "I took one of my momma's pain pills and I was knocked out cold."

"Come on nah, you couldn't have been hurting that bad."

"You try jumping up and down for three hours straight."

"You got volleyball practice tonight too," I asked.

Hope put her head back and blew out a deep breath. "Don't remind me. My legs are still hurting. And I'm starting not to like volleyball anymore."

"Hold up a minute nah. Don't get mad at the sport, 'cause volleyball is my best friend." I said, while looking down at Hope's thick thighs pushing a print together.

She playfully punched me on the arm.

The teacher came out of the boys' locker room and stood in front of the class. "Today we're going to be watching a tap dealing with STDs, sexual transmitted diseases. Once the tap starts, if you have any questions you could raise your hand at any time and I'll pause the tape to answer it or you could simply take out your notebook and write the question down then ask after the tap goes off.

Coach Harrison pressed play on the VCR then went stood on the side. Everyone stayed quiet as a black woman with a stethoscope hanging from her neck came on the screen. The doctor started talking about the different kinds of STDs that was out there. She said it was a lot of different STDs, but the most common ones are:

Syphilis

Gonorrhea

Herpes

Genital Warts

Chlamydia

HIV/AIDS

She said that Chlamydia, Syphilis, and Gonorrhea, were STDs that you could get rid of with the treatment of medicine, but the other four were none curable diseases. All diseases could be properly treated if caught in its early stages. That's why it's so important to have four check-ups a year; once every three months or at least once every six months, depending on how active you are. If you feel the need to go at any time, there should be a clinic somewhere near you.

The doctor continued to talk about it some more then the tape came to a part that showed a dick that's been affected by Syphilis.

"eeeeewwwwww," was the only thing that could be heard throughout the gym.

The shit made my eyes squinch. The nigga was fucked up. He had a green mole on his dick head with puss coming out of it. The next picture they showed made me regret that I even caught a glimpse of it. When I say the dude was tore up, that's not even the half of it. He had bumps, moles, warps, and a whole lot of other stuff all over his shit. The conclusion that I got from the glimpse was, kill ya'self.

After the tape went off and the teacher asked were there any questions, about eight hands automatically went up.

"Can you get a STD from a girl going down on you?" A dude sitting in the middle asked.

"It's not a high risk, but yes Travis, you can still catch it. Here's how it works: If a female is bleeding anywhere in her mouth, her blood would have to get into the hole of your penis, travel through it, and that's when you become infected with whatever it is that she has." Coach Harrison answered. "The risk is higher if you go down on her."

He went to one of the females that had their hand raised. "Why the Lady didn't say anything about crabs or being burnt?" She asked.

"Well Samantha, neither one of those is a STD. A boy being burnt simply goes to the clinic and the nurse or doctor stick's a long q-tip up his pee hole to drain all the stuff out. Gives him a couple of pills and send him on his way. Now here's the tricky part. A boy will know within seventy-two hours after he's come in contact with it, but a female could go weeks or even months without knowing. That's why it's good and important for you and your sex partner to communicate with each other.

Crabs are something that you catch from having sex with an unclean person. I think I heard someone say that they shaved all of their hair off from down there and scrubbed their body real good to get rid of it."

"My brother said that he took a bath in some bleach to get rid of his." Someone sitting in the front of the class blurted out.

"Well I guess that's another way of getting rid of it."
Coach Harrison said. He went to another girl that raised her
hand.

"If you're a virgin, can you catch something on your first
time?"

"What the fuck!" I said to myself, but I think Hope still
heard me.

Me and Hope didn't say anything to each other while the
class was going on. We just sat there and listened to everything.
After seeing that tape and listening to all this talk about STDs, I
hope Hope's not thinking that I might have something because
I'm straight. I can't remember the last time that I went to the
doctor, but I know I'm straight. Shit, you can just call me Mr.
Trojan Man 'cause I never leave home without it.

Class went on for a few more minutes and then the bell
ringed. School's over. Me and Hope stood across from each
other outside of the gym.

"What time volleyball practice starts?" I asked.

"Right after the buses pulls off the class gotta be in the
gym." She answered.

"Around what time you want me to call you tonight?"

"I should be there no later than six. After practice, I'm not
going to my grandma house. I'm going straight home." Hope
didn't live here in the south either. She lived close to where I live
at, but in Ghost Town. Hope's grandma lived in the south. She

used that address to go to McKinley High. McKinley High was the only school left in Baton Rouge that didn't have to wear uniforms so this the school where all the high schoolers wanted to be at.

I saw my cousin Peewee and Zeus walking towards me, "I'm coming," I told'em when they got close enough to hear me.

"Aiight," Peewee said, "We gon' be by the car."

I nodded my head while telling Peewee Aiight. The two of them walked off.

"Well come here and give me a hug," I said, while pulling Hope by the waist towards me. We hugged for around thirty seconds then when she went back and came in to give me a kiss, she damn near put me on the wall. We kissed long and hard in front of all the students around us. By the time she let me go, I felt kind of dizzy. I told her that I'll talk to her tonight and walked off feeling light headed. If I had any thoughts or wonders about if that tape had her spooked, then that kiss just eliminated it.

My grandma ended up moving from Myrtle Street to 16th Street. Right next door to my auntie's Trish house, Coon's momma. That's where either my brother or my momma came pick me up from. Some times when Trap felt like letting me stunt, he'll give me the keys to his Cut-lass Ciara and let me drive it to school. On those days I got my stunt on fa'real.

When Peewee turned on 16th Street, I hung up my cellphone while noticing Coon standing on the corner. Peewee pulled up in front of my grandma's house then all three of us got out and walked over to Coon. As we were dapping Coon down, we heard a horn blow from behind us. I turned around and saw my dog Future sitting in his Cadillac Deville on the other side of the street. Future is the person that I just got off the phone with.

I walked to his car with my book sack still on my back. After I opened the passenger door and got in, we dapped each other down.

"What up wit'cha lil' one," Future asked.

"Same thang with me big roune."

"Same thang?"

"Fa'shanks." I responded.

Future reached under his seat and pulled out the same thang that I got from him last week. At the same time, I was counting out three-hundred and sixty dollars from my bankroll. I gave Future the money in all twenty dollar bills and put what he gave me in my book sack. I zipped my book sack back then we dapped each other down again.

"Be cool out chea lil' one," Future said, as I opened the door.

"Fa'shanks my nigga. I'ma get back at cha." I said, then closed his door back.

"Aye Coon," I yelled.

Coon looked at me and started nodding his head up and down to let me know that the front door was opened. I went to his house and put my book sack in his room. When I came back out, Coon's lil' brother Roger was standing on the porch. Roger was like a year or two under my lil brother; short, like skinned, and chubby. He's been living on 16<sup>th</sup> Street his whole life, born and being raised right here in this house. Being the younger brother of Coon and having a direct insight of my life, Roger is destined for greatness.

"What up fat boy?" I walked over to Roger and threw him a jab to the rib.

"Nigga I ain't fat," He responded.

"Yes you is. What chu doing out chea?"

"Just getting off the bus," He answered.

"And like I said; what chu doing out chea? Boy you know you better get in that house and do ya homework." I said, and walked off the porch.

"Nigga you better go 'head with all that," he yelled back.

On my way back to the corner, I looked across the street and seen three dudes that I never saw around here before. They were walking in the same direction as me. I continued to look because one of them I think I have seen, but that couldn't be the same person that I thought it was. When I crossed the street, they were going in the store. My lil' cousin Tito must have just come on this side of town because he was standing there with Peewee, Zeus, and Coon. It was also two of our other rounes from off 16<sup>th</sup> posted up on the block, Crazy and Lil' Mo.

When the three dudes came out the store, I watched them as they began walking back down the street. "Man bruh, I think I know that nigga." I said aloud.

"Which one," Crazy asked.

"The tall nigga in the middle; I think that's that same clown I got into it with over in Fairfield."

"That's him," Crazy quickly said. "Come on."

We started fast walking to catch up wit'em.

Crazy took the lead. "Say, Pookie," he called out.

When Pookie turned around, Crazy signaled with his hand for Pookie to come here. Pookie met Crazy in the street at the same time that we made it to him.

"Say, don't I know you nigga," I asked.

Pookie squinched his eyes like he was studying my face. Then he shook his head no.

"You be in Fairfield?" I asked.

"My grandma live in Fairfield."

"You that same nigga me and my dog Fred got into it with over there."

He continued to shake his head.

"Man that's that nigga Toine," Crazy yelled.

When I hit him with a quick right to the left side of his face, he went back a step or two. I was going in to finish the job, but Tito came and hit him from behind. Pookie turned around and started running, leaving one of his shoes behind. I went over and picked it up.

"You know where that go," Crazy said, pointing to the top of an abandon building; where it went.

Pookie got down the street and started talking shit as he back peddled away. We went stood back in front of the Yang's. Crazy told us that Pookie had just moved down the street. How he knew that that was the same nigga I was talking about is because as soon as I mentioned something about Fairfield, he knew that's where all Pookie's people lived, so that had to be the same nigga. He also said that Pookie's people was Bacchus and Barlow, which was two known head busting brothers from out of Fairfield, so be prepared.

"Cool," I responded.

When we heard the sound of thunder nearby, we all turned our heads and saw the blue Navigator sitting on 24's hit the corner.

Ivy Smith, aka Jersey Phat, aka Da Don, aka Da Real Bird Man. He's from 16th Street too. When I was younger, I used to see him all the time posted up right here in front of the Yang's. That was back in 1992 when we used to live up the street in the brown house, before my momma met the pastor, got married, and moved us to the bottom with him.

The birdman hasn't been around for a while because he's been doing time in the feds. He just came home not even a month ago and already he's one of the biggest niggas in the city. His lil' brother told me that he put the cost of a Bentley on his teeth; screwed in platinum and diamonds. Besides from a nigga from out the Park, who goes by the name of Tulu, wasn't anybody down here seeing the kind of paper as Lil' Ivy.

Lil' Ivy stopped his truck in front of the Yang's and let his lil' brother Tavoris out. Tavoris is a twin, but his twin brother is locked up at the moment. After Lil' Mo went took Tavoris place on the passenger seat, Lil' Ivy pulled off.

"Toine, how long you gon' be over here," My cousin Zeus asked.

"I don't know," I answered, "my momma or Trap prolly on their way now."

"Oh, because Peewee bout to drop me off by my grandma house, I was gon' pass back over here to see if you was still out chea." Zeus replied.

"Yea just pass back through." I told him. "They prolly don't come until later on sometime, ain't no telling."

"Aiight," Zeus said, then came over and gave me some dap.

"Tell your brother I said hit me up." Peewee told me as he dapped me down too.

Zeus is one of the Shepherds. He's related to them on his daddy side of the family. He got their last name and all. When he said that he was going to his grandma house, he was talking about his grandma on his daddy side, Faith.

-CHAPTER 13-

Over the last eighteen months, Jon-Jon and the Shepherds shine came through hard. Even though they had to pay draft to Da Birdman Ivy Smith which was thirty-five thousand dollars every first of the month for the next five years, they still took in a damn good amount for themselves. Jon-Jon had finally come across the kind of money that he's been trying to get since age 11. Him, Brian Shepherd, Lil' Wick Shepherd, and another hustler by the name of Phat Pat, all stood on 15th Street smoking indo blunts as they watched the smokers detail their top of the line rides.

Jon-Jon had a platinum color S500 series Benz, cleaner than a whistle. Brian had a RX Jag off the showroom floor. Lil' Wick upgraded his Old School Cadillac to a New School 1999 Fleetwood and he upgraded his 20" Dayton's to some 22's. Phat Pat had a Lexus Jeep sitting on some 21" Stars. What can I say, the game been good to'em.

"Y'all niggas think I'm acting an ass now, wait till the Mardi Gras Parade in two weeks." Lil' Wick said. "Boy I'ma be in that Five Star Hotel bungee jumping in them hoes pussy."

"You, boy I'ma pop me one of them chewies and do the fool." Phat Pat added. "Jon-Jon you got the tickets yet?"

After Jon-Jon didn't answer, Phat Pat said his name louder. "Jon-Jon!"

"Nigga don't you see me on the phone?" Jon-Jon said, pulling his cell phone away from his ear.

"What, nigga if don't wanna be disturbed then you better take ya ass up the street." Phat Pat said. "You got the tickets or what?"

Jon-Jon snapped his fingers two times to get Sharlene's attention. Sharlene was Jon-Jon's favorite smoker. She was the only smoker that he would let get close to his car, let alone clean it. He told Sharlene to grab the papers on the inside of the passenger door where she was cleaning then he went back to talking to the lil' chic that he was on the phone with before Phat Pat rudely interrupted him. After Sharlele got the papers, Phat Pat walked over to her and she hand them to him.

"You see, this is why Jon-Jon is, my, nigga!" Phat Pat said after reading his name on one of the tickets.

Brian and Lil' Wick walked over to Phat Pat.

"Yeeeeaaaa, Daytona that thang niggggaaa!" Lil' Wick said, after he read his name on one.

The reason why they had to wait until Jon-Jon got the tickets for them is because Jon-Jon was the only one with the hookup. The lil' chic, Carla, who he was now on the phone with was a flight attendant for the Metro Airport. She could get however many round trip tickets she wanted for half price. Even though all of them were paid niggas, they still looked for the cheapest way out.

## -CHAPTER 14-

(Monique)

Since the last time we talked, my life has really changed; some for the good and some for the worst. I'll start with the good stuff. Well, I got a car. Hell, I got a car, some new furniture, new clothes and jewelry. Thanks to Lester. It seems as if Lester has had money all along. Well that's what his mouth said. He said that I should've known that he had money and that he's been hustling too long for him not to have a stash somewhere. The only reason he didn't tell me sooner is because he knew that one day he would get locked up again.

He went on to say, "I wanted to see if you would stick by ya man side, through incarceration and all, and still be able to do things for me without my help. You my ride or die chic huh?"

And my response was, "Oh that's why hun?"

"Of course, what other reason would I have to keep something like this from you?"

"Lester, you ain't think about that excuse at all huh? You must've just came in here and freestyle that." Lester then put his head down. "Nigga you better go run that bullshit on one of those other bitches out there. I'm from the projects."

I know one thing, the only way for him and Carl to come up with all this money out the blue is if they robbed somebody or some place. And I don't know where the hell is Troy. I haven't seen him since Precious birthday party three weeks ago. Carl is around here riding in a drop top Z-28 Camaro; rims, T.V's, music system, the whole nine yards. And Lester went out and bought a money green Dodge Ram Pickup Truck. Then that truck is fresh from the dealership. When he first drove it to the house, it had thirty-six miles on it. The tags were still in the window and all. I bet they went and robbed somebody, but why in the hell is he keeping it from me. He acting like I'd rat on my own man.

But anyway, he got me a used Honda Accord. He said that it was something just for me to learn how to drive in. I drove it out the yard once, but that's the farthest I ever got. And if it was left up to me to drive it back in the driveway, it would've stayed right there in the middle of the street because I wasn't getting back behind that wheel. Reluctantly, Lester drove it back. Then he got the nerves to get mad at me because I don't wanna learn how to drive. Ain't that's somethin'. If I don't wanna drive then I don't wanna drive. That's my business not his.

Lester ass has been getting mad a whole lot lately which is part of the bad news I had to tell you. Since he came across this money, things between us have really changed for the worst. He barely comes home anymore, and whenever he does, he's either high or drunk; most of the time both. Every time I try to talk to him about it it's always ending in a big argument where he'll leave the house and be gone for no telling how long. The way things are going with us, there's no telling where this relationship will be tomorrow or whenever the next time I see him.

The other bad news is that I found out the reason Tonya moved back with her parents wasn't because she was missing her kids, but because she wanted to spend her last days here on earth with them. My girl Tonya is HIV positive. Me and Evet went to see her in the hospital last night and we couldn't even tell it was her. Tonya looked just that bad. She prolly weighed no more than 70 pounds. We stayed there for about an hour and talked to her. She told us that she didn't know who she had gotten it from or how long she's been having it.

The way that she found out was through a common cold, the cold just never went away. After two weeks of her trying to fight it off with some Nyquil and even flu medicine, she finally called her momma and told her that she needed to go to the hospital. That's when they told her that she's been infected the HIV Virus and that she only had a year, at the most, to live. I made a promise to her that I'd try to help her momma out with her daughters as much as possible. Evet made the same. Just thinking about those three girls brings tears to my eyes all over again. Before we left the hospital, we talked to her doctor to try and found out why the disease affected her so quick. I know somebody that's been having it for ten years now and he still look the same way he did in high school.

We found Dr. Kazase and he told us, "HIV is a complicated virus that uses RNA, not DNA, as its genetic messenger. It reproduces primarily in specialized cells of the body's immune system called CD4 Lymphocytes. During HIV replication, the CD4

~ 146 ~

cells are destroyed. As more and more cells are killed, the body loses the ability to fight off many infections. Take your friend Ms. Grea for instance: Ms. Grea number of CD4 cells falls below 200 per cubic millimeter. A lot of people like Ms. Grea don't come in until it's too late. The disease has begun destroying their CD4 cells and makes the immune system so week that when they end up with a common cold, their body's not able to fight it off with over the counter medicine. They come here and we give them the proper pills that they should have been taking a long time ago. The medicine we give them fights off the cold and buy's them some time but not much. Whenever a person CD4 cells falls below 200 per cubic millimeter, their HIV has become full blown AIDS."

Surprisingly, somebody's car pulled up to the house. I could hear the car door open and close. I remained in bed with Precious laying besides me. When Lester came into the room, I took one look at him and knew things were about to get ugly. I saw that he went out and bought himself some jewelry; three gold chains and a gold watch. The clothes he was wearing I had never seen them before either, but his eyes, they were blood shot red. His skin looked like it haven't been touched by soap and water in a week, which was prolly the last time he seen a bed, to sleep at least. Lester stood in the doorway and looked at me for a moment then he went over to the dresser. After he opened the drawl, he moved some clothes around in it for a minute then closed it back and went to the closet. The baby was sleeping, so I grabbed her and took her to her room and laid her in the crib. I quietly closed the door as I left out the room.

"Lester we need to talk." I said, as I came back into my room and closed the door.

"Where my shit at," Lester asked, while continuing to pull down stuff from the top of the closet.

"What?"

"Where my shit at?"

"Boy what in the hell are you talking about?"

Lester ignored me and continued to tear up the top of the closet in search for God knows what. "Lester if you tell me what you lost then maybe I could help you find it."

After a few moments, he stopped, put his head down, and started massaging his eyes lids with his right hand. Then he began laughing to his self.

"Can we please talk?" I asked.

Lester then turned around and pulled me to him by my waist while forcing his lips on mines.

"No Lester. We need to talk." I managed to pry my lips from his to say.

He continued to kiss me on my face and neck while pulling up my night gown and grabbing a hand full of ass. He knew damn well that I wouldn't have on any panties; only time I wore those to bed is when I had to. I tried to pull away from him, but he was just determined to have his way. Without pausing or loosening the strong hold he held of me with his left arm, with his right hand he pulled a gun from out of his waist band then reached over to put it on the dresser. Today was Friday, and luckily, I let J.J and Jonathan spent the weekend by Crystal. Lester planned on accomplishing his goal, whether I wanted to or not, so after we fell on the bed, with him on top, I stopped fighting.

-CHAPTER 15-

(Antoine)

It's a Saturday morning, and I'm sitting under the tree on 16$^{th}$ and Bynum trying not to be seen by the whole neighborhood. Trap had dropped me off over here about thirty minutes ago before he went to work. Trap works at Exxon Plant making eighteen dollars an hour. Now that's what I call good money. After taxes, he still brings home over a grand every week. Not to mention if he works overtime which is something he does on the regular. No bullshitting, that nigga checks be looking like thirteen-hundred and sixty something dollars with some change left over. Man that's what's up, especially when you're just turning eighteen. You see, Trap is not really what you would call a street nigga. He's been having a job ever since he was fourteen years old. Don't get me wrong, he could fight his ass off plus he still likes all the things that your average hustler would like; money, cars, and clothes. He just never sold any drugs to get it.

As I was looking up the street, I saw my dog Jonny come out of his auntie's house. I watched him as he got inside of his light blue Jag. As he began driving, I stood up and came into view. He stopped in front of me. I went around the car then opened the passenger door and got in.

"Jonnyyy," I said, as we slapped and gripped each other's hand.

In case you're wondering who Jonny is, not only was he my dude from school, but he was also my producer's lil' brother. Yea you heard me. Wasn't anymore hoping and dreaming about seeing the inside of a studio because me and Jonny damn near lived in one. Toine, aka 50 Flames, became the latest member of "Everythang Raw Records".

"50 flames, how it's going down?" Jonny asked.

"You know me, staying below the radar." I responded.

As Jonny drove, we seen that it had a few people out, but because it was still kind of chilly, all the females were in the house. All we saw was a bunch of hard legs standing outside in pants, jackets, and hoods. Me and Jonny talked about different stuff, but mainly about studio business. Jonny blocked for about an hour and a half around the whole South Side, from the top to the bottom. When he turned back on 16$^{th}$ Street, we saw four people standing on the corner in front of the store; Yang Gang. I quickly recognized them as Roynell, Coon, Crazy, and Lil' Mo. Roynell is another one of my cousins. Do you remember my cousin Big Luck, who came and picked me up from Monique's house that day when I went back home? Well Roynell and Big Luck are brothers. Jonny stopped in front of the Yang's. Before I got out he asked if I would be ready for next weekend. We had a concert to do that his brother booked for us at Club Zone.

"Come on nah Jonny; I'm ready now." I told him, then dapped him down.

"Hit me up." He yelled, as I got out.

"Fa'shanks my nigga," I yelled back, before closing his door.

"Did somethin' come through for me," I asked Roynell, as I walked up to him.

Around this time, there were only two people on 16<sup>th</sup> that sold weed. That was me and our big dog Dirty Red. Everybody else served hard.

"I'm just coming out my damn self cuz." Roynell responded.

"How long you been on this side?" Coon asked me.

"'Bout an hour," I answered. "You got that book sack I put on your porch?"

"It's in my room," Coon answered.

As I was looking toward the end of the street, I saw two dudes come walking from off of South Blvd. When they got halfway to us, I realized that it was my dog Fred. I started walking towards him. I didn't know the dude that Fred was with, but I figured that it was somebody from off of Fred's street which was 12<sup>th</sup> Street.

"Something told me that you were on this side," Fred said, as he initiated the greeting. "What's up wit'cha?"

"I'm cooling roune," I answered. "What's the deal?"

~ 152 ~

"Aye they got this nigga over there selling a Desert Eagle." Fred responded.

"For how much," I asked.

"The nigga say he wants a bill twenty-five, but chu could prolly talk'em down."

"He's still over there?"

"Yea," Fred answered. "He live right there across the tracks."

"Come show me."

We started walking to the dude's house which was literally right around the corner. When Fred knocked on the door, a slim dude with brads in his head opened it. I looked at him and knew that this wasn't my first time seeing him. Actually I've seen him a lot. Passing down 16th Street in a beige color De Nova, which is the same car that was parked outside. He let us in and Fred tells him that I wanted to check out that thang. Without hesitation, he left the living room and went in one of the back rooms. After a few moments, he came back with one of the prettiest guns that I had ever seen in my life; all chrome, wood handle, big, and would make a nigga get right. I didn't show him any facial expressions, but once I took one look at that gun, I knew I couldn't leave without it.

"Seventeen shot Desert Eagle," He said, and pulled out the clip, cocked it back, and a bullet came flying out the chamber. He caught the slug with his right hand then hand me the gun.

Damn it's heavy; I thought to myself. "How much you

want for it?" I asked after a few moments of checking it out.

"One-forty," He answered; trying to jack somethin'.

"I'm straight," I said, while handing the gun back to him.

"Give me one twenty-five then," He corrected his self without getting the gun out of my hand.

I took my time thinking about it while looking the gun over.

"Aye you got the weed on 16th huh?" He asked, but already knew I did. "Give me three and a half ounces."

That ain't gon' happen. "Shit, I need to re-up now." I went in my pocket and pulled out my bankroll. I went ahead and gave him the bill twenty-five that he wanted. He gave me the clip then started counting the money.

"You got some more bullets for it?" I asked, while putting the clip in.

"Nah uh," He answered, "But that's a full clip though."

He had already put the bullet that he made fly out of the chamber back into the clip. He left from out of the living room again.

"When you get ready, I got this thang for sell too." He said, as he came back into the living room and raised a gun into the air that was prolly the same size as my leg. "This a SKS Assault Rifle." He took out the banana clip then put it back in and cocked the gun back.

~ 154 ~

LATER ON THAT NIGHT everybody from 16$^{th}$ street was on Bynum Street shooting dice by Ms. Brenda's house. We chose to shoot there because Ms. Brenda's house was the closest one to us that had a concrete porch. We started off only shooting a light two bet three, which only lasted for ten minutes. Big Head was the first one to get tired of it so he started singing aloud,

"Shoot yo nickel,

shoot yo nickel, shoot yo nickel.

Bet yo nickel,

bet yo nickel, bet yo nickel."

Big Head was remixing Jadakiss's, "We gonna make it," ft. Styles P. Everybody started singing along with him as we raised the pot to shoot five and bet five, ten, or whatever.

Big Head was a rapper also. He had just signed with Trill ENT., which was the same record company that signed another rapper from out of South Baton Rouge by the name of Lil' Boosie. Lil' Boosie is the same artiste that used to rap for the Concentration Camp, which was owned by an entrepreneur from out of Baton Rouge who goes by the name of, C-Loc.

When it was my turn to shoot, I shook the dice up real good and rolled out two fives. "A ten, my favorite point," I said, and went around betting everybody ten and twenty dollars. I dropped a twenty to my fader, which totaled up to fifty dollar between just me and him. I scanned all the money around the board and quickly estimated that this was a hundred fifty dollar pot. I grabbed the dice and shook'em up real good again then rolled out two duces. Ten's running mate. The next shot I rolled out was a nine.

"Aiight," I said, and picked the dice up again and shot'em out one by one. We call this t-laying the dice; playing with the dice trying to put them on a number that you felt comfortable shootin' them off of. I t-layed them a couple of times until they fell on two duces then I picked the dice up and shot'em out without shaking them. The dice landed on a duce and a five.

"Fuck," I said, as I watched everybody picking up my money. I was so pissed off at missing that point that I didn't even hear my cell phone ringing. Tavoris waved his hand to get my attention then he pointed to my side. I looked down and seen the red light blinking. I grabbed my sprint pcs and flipped it opened then looked at the number on the screen before I pressed the talk button. "Yea."

"Hey. Why you ain't been answering your phone?" Ebony asked.

Ebony is somebody that I met when I was going Valley Park Alternative School last year. She couldn't compare to my girl Hope. Ebony had a caramel complexion, slim, decent face, and some long curly hair. Her ass was kind of flat, but she had some big gorgeous breast. I knew my girl Hope was a good girl and all, but we been together for six months and I still ain't hit. Not that I was pressing her or anything. Shit, I haven't even brought it up to her. I was playing my cards all the way right. The main reason I was messing with Ebony was simply because it was convenient. She lived on Matilda Street which was two blocks away from 16<sup>th</sup> so whenever I was on this side, which was most of the time anyway, I could chill by her house.

"Mane I'm busy," I said into the phone. "I'm trying to get this money out chea." I dropped a twenty dollar bill to my back man.

"Ok, I was just calling to see if I was gon' see you tonight." Ebony said.

"Yea," I answered. "I'ma call you when I get through with this."

"Alright," She responded.

I closed my phone and put it back in the case then got back into what I was doing.

After the game was over, the result came out to be the same way that it's been for the past two weeks. Crazy broke it up. I ain't gon' lie; Crazy is one of the luckiest niggas alive when it comes to gambling. I never seen or even heard of him losing before. I won some of the money back that I had lost. At first, I was losing two hundred, but I shook back and only lost thirty.

While I was sitting on the wooden box in front of the Yang's, counting money, Tavoris walked up to me and asked if I wanted to go half on a fifth of Hennessy.

"Aiight," I said. Knowing that a fifth cost $27.99, I handed Tavoris fifteen dollars. Instead of getting the money from me, he hand me his fifteen dollars. "I can't buy it," I told him.

"What she put you out too?" He asked. Momma Yang's stopped damn near the whole 16th Street from going in her store.

"Nah I can go in, but I'm fifteen years old. She ain't gon' let me buy alcohol from out there."

"Shit," He said, and got the fifteen dollars from me.

After a couple of minutes of us waiting for somebody to come, who was old enough to buy liquor and could actually go in the store, Lil' Wick Shepherd pulled on side of the Yang's. Lil' Wick got out of his Cadillac and left it running with the fifteens banging. Before he went in the store, he walked up to twin and dapped him down. In return, Twin gave him the money for the Hennessy.

"What this foe?" Lil' Wick asked.

"Get a fifth of Hennessy from out there." Twin told him.

"Can't none of y'all niggas out chea go in the stoe?" Lil' Wick asked, looking around at all the niggas posted up. He then busted out laughing. "Boy that don't make no damn sense. Y'all niggas stay with the flat bullshit around here."

After Lil' Wick came back out the store, he hand the Hennessey to twin then got back in his car and busted out. Twin came and gave me the bottle; giving me the honors of popping it open. An hour later, we was drunk and ordering another one before the store closed at 12:00. It was only me and twin drinking. Everybody else was doing their own thang. Twin didn't smoke weed because I think he was on papers. I must've smoked about a half of ounce damn near by myself. My cousin Roynell came and hit the weed a few times. Coon took it in about an hour ago. Coon wouldn't really a night person. After Roynell got high, he took it in too. Roynell lived at the house with my

~ 158 ~

grandma. Before we knew it, me and twin were the only two people left on 16<sup>th</sup>. Since we were both on the same level, we tripped off each other. When I couldn't take no more, I looked over to where twin was sitting on the porch of Ms. Brenda's house and seen, I think, about a quarter left in the bottle.

"Twin I'm out," I said. I must've been talking to myself 'cause in my blurry vision of twin, his head was leaning back in the chair and his eyes were closed. I got up and started walking, well, staggling down the street.

# -CHAPTER 16-

(Antoine)

"Wake up.  Toine, wake up."

"I felt somebody constantly pushing me.  Then the sound of Ebony's nagging voice calling my name.  "What," I said without opening my eyes.

"Toine, get up."  She repeated.

I strained my eyes to open and I got them halfway there, which was enough for me to see Ebony sitting in the bed with her arms folded across her chest and her face all frowned up.  "Mane what chu want; waking me up."  I complained.

"Toine get up."

"Mane I'm up!"

"No, Toine get up."

"I'm up," I said, and wrapped my arm around her legs, where her body was supposed to be.  Ebony had on what she usually wore to bed; a t-shirt and some panties.  I laid my head on her thighs.

"Toine, don't you ever come over here like that again."

"What chu talking 'bout?" I asked.

"You know what I'm talking 'bout; coming over here all drunk."

"Oh, you could tell?" I asked, still not able to keep my eyes opened.

"Toine, you threw up on me."

I couldn't help but to bust out laughing.

"That shit ain't funny," Ebony said, and slapped me in the back of my head. "My shirt over there full up with ya nasty throw up."

"Damn, my bad ma."

"What chu was drinking last night 'cause you don't ever need to drink that again? And what chu got a gun for? It's not like you could've used it if somebody wanted to do you something."

"Where my gun at," I asked.

"I put it in the drawl."

"What time is it," I peeped and saw the sunlight coming in the room through the window.

"You can't open your eyes and see that big ass clock on the dresser? It's 1:28." Ebony answered.

"Your grandma in there?"

"She left thirty minutes ago and went to the store."

Ebony's house was like my second home. I had clothes, a couple pair of shoes, boxers; toothbrush and all over there.

"Go turn the shower on for me." I told her.

"After what chu put me through last night, I ought to be telling you to go run me some water. You better go do it ya'self."

I turned my head and acted like I was about to bite her on the leg. Ebony jumped when she felt my teeth. She slid her body under the covers with mine's.

"Toine, open your eyes."

I opened my eyes halfway again and seen her face inches away from mine's. Ebony made a fits with her small hand and put it in my face. "I'ma beat chu up if you come over here like that again." She threatened.

"You took care of me last night?"

"Toine what chu was drinking?"

"Me and twin just had some Hennessy."

"How much did y'all have?"

"I don't know."

"Well, you don't need to drink no more of that because you wouldn't right."

"You'll run me some water," I asked again.

Ebony got up from the bed and went to the front of the

house. I heard her close her grandma room door then go into the bathroom. As the sound of the shower came on, I reached down on the side of the bed for my pants. I got the pants and went in the pockets, but I didn't find what I was looking for. When I raised my head, I noticed it sitting on the table next to the bed.

I grabbed my cellphone, thinking to myself, "I know Ebony went through my shit." I flipped it opened and confirmed my beliefs. I had no missed calls. I went in the recent calls section then clicked on received calls. I had two unanswered calls from a 357-5611 number. Hope's number. One call came in at 11:16pm, and the other at 12:02am.

"I see you don't know how to keep ya hands to ya'self huh?" I asked Ebony, as soon as she came back into the room.

She got back in the bed and put her face all close to mine's again. "Who's calling you from that 357-5611 number?"

"Don't go in my shit again."

"Who is that Toine?"

"None of ya business. You go in my shit again and I'ma kick ya ass."

"Well, just tell none-of-my-business not to be calling you at 11 and 12:00 at night." Ebony said.

I got up and went to the dresser to get some boxers out.

"I put a towel on the toilet for you already," Ebony said.

I walked out without responding.

When I came back in the room Ebony was sitting up in the

~ 163 ~

bed watching TV. I walked to the closet and got out a fresh pair black Girbauds pants along with my red, white, and black Hawaii Fubu shirt, then reached on top of the closet for my fresh pair of Soulja Reebok's that I only wore once. I sat on the bed and got dressed.

"I know you ain't mad 'cause I went in your phone," Ebony said.

"Fa'real mane, don't go in my shit again." I restated.

"Oh my God," Ebony said while laughing. "I can't believe he mad at me and he's the one with a bitch calling him."

"Fuck that! I don't go in ya shit."

"You could go in mine's. It's right there on the dresser."

After I was fully dressed, I went and grabbed my pants from off the floor. I dug in all the pockets and transferred everything to the ones I had on.

"You think your grandma would take you to the cleaners?" I asked.

Ebony nodded her head up and down, "Whenever she come back."

I gave Ebony two twenty dollar bills and told her to put two pair of my pants in the cleaners for me. I went and grabbed my cell phone from off the dresser then opened the drawl and got that thang out. Ebony got up and followed me to the back door. The same door I always used. After I went out, I walked down two of the three steps there were then turned around. She stood at the top step with the door still opened.

"What chu finna do," I asked.

"I'ma wait for my grandma to come back so I can put your clothes in the cleaners for you then I prolly go by Candice house for a lil' bit." Candice was her friend that lived in the house next door. Candice was cold bloody; red bone, titties big like Ebony's but Candice had ass too, cute face and all. I tried to put a couple of my cousins on her, but couldn't none of'em hit. They all chilled with her and probably smoked weed and talked to her for a couple of days, but all of them told me the same thing. "Mane that girl is crazy behind that nigga of hers. That's all she ever wanna talk about."

"Alight, I'ma just hit chu up later on then." I told her and she shook her head up and down. I gave her a hug then turned around and left.

When I got back on 16$^{th}$, the only person I seen outside was Dirty Red. I ain't worry about bringing my cellphone charger over here because Coon had the same kind of phone as me. I went to his house. His lil' sister Dasia answered the door.

"What's up Das?" I asked.

"Shit," She said, and moved to the side. Coon's room was all the way in the back of the house. When I went in it he was laying on his bed watching Scarface, a movie that will never go out of style.

"You're still laying down nigga?" I asked.

"Shit cuz I'm tired. Amy ass kept me on the phone till 1:00 this morning." Coon answered.

Coon's girl Amy:  You know my cousin Coon was the only one in the family with a white girlfriend.  Me myself, I never messed with one before.  Not that I have anything against white girls.  Matter of fact, I wouldn't mind having one if me and Hope wouldn't together, and it was only for a night or two.  I gave Coon the Desert Eagle and told him to put it up for me until tonight then I connected my cellphone to his charger that was plugged into the wall next to his bed and went outside.

"Big roune, how it's going down out chea," Walking up on the curve, I approached the big homie with love.  Dirty Red was like another Big Mike except Dirty Red was in his early thirties; an OG from his red bald head to his feet.  Dirty Red was the only person that I had ever seen with thirty-two gold teeth.  The only person that I ever even heard about having that many was Baby from Cash Money.  You remember that video with Cash Money and Three Six Mafia where Baby said, "Juvy got 4 and B.G. got 10, but with my 32 golds playboy we all in"?  Other than those two, the most niggas was getting was either 12 or 18.  I kicked it with Dirty Red and got some of that street knowledge that he educate all the hustles around here with.

After about an hour, Coon came outside with my cellphone in his hands.  He gave it to me then told me that Monique said to call her.

"She called on my phone?"  I asked, grabbing the phone from him and clicking on the recent calls.

"Nah uh," Coon answered.  "It's finished charging.  I think she want chu to watch them kids for her tonight."

"Oh, she prolly wanna go to Playboy's," I said.  "What's

the number?"

Coon grabbed the phone from out of my hand and started dialing numbers. "He said he'll do it," Coon said into the phone. "I'm serious woman. I wouldn't lie to you. This is his phone I'm calling you off of."

I already knew that Monique first asked Coon to babysit for her and he was putting it off on me, with his slick ass. I wouldn't tripping though. Monique was just like a second mom to me, so whenever she needed me, if I was able to, I tried to be there for her.

Coon hand the phone back to me. "She wanna talk to you."

"Yea its cool Monique," I said.

"Alright, I was just making sho 'cause Coon be lying so much," Monique said. "What time you gon' be over here?"

"You're going to playboys at nine, right." I asked.

"Yeah," She answered.

"I'ma be over there at like eight or eight-thirty."

"Alright, thank you too Antoine."

"Aiight Monique," I said and closed my phone.

"Coon nigga you think you slick. I know she asked you first." I said.

Coon started laughing. "Mane bruh, I don't be feeling like watching those kids; Jonathan bad ass gon' make me beat the shit outta him."

"There he goooo," I said, as Tito came up to me and gave me some dap. "You just coming over here?"

"Yea, I just jumped off the city bus." Tito answered. "How long you been on this side?"

"Since yesterday," I answered. "I'm not gon' bust out until tomorrow though. Monique asked me to babysit for her tonight."

"You not going to school in the morning?" Tito asked.

"Yea I'm going," I told him. "I got some clothes in my book sack over by Coon's house."

"Aye, what's up with Alexis?" Tito asked, referring to one of Ebony's friends. "You think she gon' be with Ebony tonight?"

"I can call Ebony and set something up," I said.

"Yea do that, bring them hoes by Monique's." Tito said.

"How you gon' get back home tonight," I asked.

"Monique would let me spend the night, as long as you over there," Tito said. "I'll just catch the city bus back home in the morning."

"Aiight," I said, and grabbed my cellphone because it was almost that time.

When me and Tito got to Monique's house, J.J came and opened the door for us. Monique was in the bathroom with the door opened.

"What's up Monique," I asked, standing in the hallway outside the bathroom.

"Hey Antoine," Monique spoke back, while still looking in the mirror and doing her hair. "You don't have to do anything with J.J or Jonathan because they already ate and took their bath. Precious is in her room sleeping, but if she wakes up then all you have to do is give her a bottle and she'll go right back to sleep."

"What's going on Monique," Tito said, coming from out of the living room into the hallway.

"Hey Tito," Monique responded. "How's your momma doing?"

"She cooling," Tito answered.

We heard the front door opened then the sound of Evet's loud voice. "Bitch you ready," Evet asked, coming into the small hallway where me and Tito was standing. Both of us spoke to her then she asked me where my momma was.

"She at the crib," I answered, as me and Tito walked passed her and went in the living room.

A couple moments later, Evet and Monique came in the living room. "I doubt it if Lester come, but if he does then you could just tell'em that I went to the club." Monique said, as she grabbed her purse from off the kitchen counter and put it on her shoulder.

I got up from the couch and followed them to the front door. "And thank you again Antoine," Monique said. "I'm not gon' be out too late."

"Aiight," I said, and locked the door behind them.

I went sat back on the couch and grabbed the house phone from off the night stand. I had only talked to my girl one time today, and that was earlier after I left Ebony's house. Keeping it one hundred, I was missing her like crazy.

"Hello," The sound of an angel.

"Hey boo bear."

"Hey baby. What took you so long to call me back?" Hope asked.

"After I got off the phone wit' chu earlier, I had to go by Coon's house and put the phone on the charger. I forgot my charger at home."

"Uhm and what happened to you last night?"

Damn I hated lying to my girl, but what I hated more than that was her being mad at me. "Me and Tito started drinking last night. One bottle led to two and two bottles led to me being drunk. I passed out right here on my auntie's couch." Fuck! Felt like every time I lied to her I was shooting myself in the foot.

Hope laughed from hearing about me being drunk, I guess, but I knew she didn't believe that shit. Hope had a big brother name Leo that graduated from McKinley High last year. I knew she seen him doing some of the same stuff that I was trying to do, so she had to be on top of me. Hope was just one of those real kind hearted people. I never before even heard her raise her voice. Not even when I did things to try and make her mad.

I stayed on the phone with Hope for around forty-five minutes then I told her that I was going to the store right quick, digging the whole deeper and deeper. If it wasn't for Tito, I wouldn't even have messed with Ebony that night. Ebony didn't usually see me for no two nights in a row, and I never before neglected Hope for two nights back to back either. We said our "I love yous" and I ended the call with me promising that I would call her when I got back. And that was a promise that I planned to keep.

After I put the phone back on the hook, I went checked on Precious. I opened the door to her room and she was wide awake, standing up in her crib in the dark. I cut on the light and she just stared at me. "I thought you were supposed to be sleep," I said. I went and picked her up from out of the baby's crib and I didn't see any dried up tears on her face. I guess she was content with being in the dark.

On our way to the kitchen, to get her a bottle from out the refrigerator, Tito asked, "Why you woke her up?"

"This girl was wide awake in there." I told him. "Just let her suck on this and she'll be sound asleep in no time." I said, coming back into the living room and handing the baby along with the bottle to Tito. "I'm 'bout to go get Ebony them."

"Mane bruh don't be long Toine," Tito complained, while putting Precious bottle in her mouth, "Fa'real man."

"I ain't nigga," I said.

Tito sat back on the couch and got back into the movie "Blade two" that was showing on Monique's digital cable box. I grabbed my cellphone to call Ebony as I walked out the door.

When I got up the street from Ebony's house, I noticed her and Alexis sitting on the back of Ebony's grandpa Buick Riviera. They got down started walking my way.

Ebony had on a red tube top with some blue jean pants and a brand new pair of all white low top Reebok Classic. She had her long curly hair pulled back into a ponytail. Like I said before, Ebony is far from ugly. Really and truly, she looked damn good. Somebody else probably would've made her his main old lady. I probably would have too, if Hope wouldn't Hope.

"What's up ma," I asked, while giving Ebony a hug.

"Nothing," she responded.

"What's up Lex?" I gave Alexis a half of hug. You know the kind of hug that a guy does with a chic that he's real cool with. The two stands sideways and the dude put one arm around the girl's shoulders and she put both of hers around his waist. Well that's the kind of hug me and Alexis did. Alexis was my dog fa'real. And when I say dog, I mean that literally. Alexis was a baby pit bull. She stood at no more than four feet eight inches and weighed prolly ninety-five pounds flat, but she could fight her ass off. I've seen Alexis lil' ass whoop some of the biggest bitches.

"Toine, how far does your auntie stay?" Ebony asked, already nagging me.

"Not far," I told her, "Just right across Government Street; on the other side of 16$^{th}$."

I looked at my watch and seen that it was 10:52 pm. It

wouldn't that many people outside; only a few on the street that we were walking down which was 15$^{th}$ Street. Because it was a Sunday, all the corner stores around here closed at 10:30 pm. The streets looked almost deserted. We got to the corner of 15$^{th}$ and South Blvd and turned right so that we could take 16$^{th}$ to 17$^{th}$ then cut through the ally and come out right in front of Monique's house. When we came to the corner of South Blvd and 16$^{th}$, we looked behind us and noticed a car sitting at the corner of 15$^{th}$ and South Blvd. We turned on 16$^{th}$. Not too long after, that same car turned on 16$^{th}$. The driver hit the brakes real hard, stopping onside of us. Me, Ebony, and Alexis stopped walking and looked at the car.

Pookie and two of his boys jumped out. My fist was already balled and I was in my kick-ass-stand when Pookie ran up. I side stepped to the left and swung at him with my right hand. My punch didn't really connect with him like I wanted it to. I only hit his hands. His other two boys ran up on me.

"Don't crowd him," Alexis said.

I was standing where I could see all three of them, but Pookie kept trying to walk around me so he could catch me from behind. When Pookie got by Alexis, who was standing on the side with Ebony, Alexis jumped up and snuck the piss outta Pookie. The other two rushed me at the same time. I swung a couple more punches at them then I turned around and took off running. We were only a few houses down from Coon and my grandma house. I heard the driver of the car that Pookie them jumped out of, who was some fat chick that never got out, screamed, "He going get a gun!"

"Fuck, Fuck, Fuck, Fuck," I cursed at myself for not getting my gun back from Coon this evening as I ran between the two houses. I went behind my grandma house and reached under the steps then quickly ran back out. Ebony and Alexis had made it to the front of Coon's house by the time I ran from out the backyard.

"Look at that big ole gun," Alexis said.

"Which way they went," I asked, then cocked the SKS as I ran by them.

16$^{th}$ is a one-way street, so I ran down it the only way they could have went, while looking down all the side streets. After I looked down prolly too many, I turned around and started walking toward Pookie's house.

"Go home," I said, walking in the middle of the street as I passed by Ebony and Alexis who was walking on the side walk. I went stood on the corner of 16$^{th}$ and Terrance; a couple houses down from where Pookie lived. Not too long after, I looked up the street and saw Coon walking towards me.

"These bitch ass niggas just tried to crowd me," I told Coon, when he finally reached me.

"How many of'em," He asked.

"Three," I said. "Them niggas ain't in that house yet because I would've seen that car passed."

"So what you gon' do my nigga," Coon asked.

"Nigga as soon as I see the headlights of that fucking car, I'ma rip that bitch to pieces!"

"Toine," Ebony was calling me from the corner of 16$^{th}$ and

South Blvd.

"Man I told her to take her stupid ass home," I said. I ain't gon' lie, as mad as I was at that moment, I felt sorry for the wrong car that just so happen to pass down one of the four streets that my eyes kept traveling back and forth on.

"Toine, the police coming!" Ebony yelled.

Me and Coon struck out running in between the two houses we were standing in front of. I threw the chopper under the house to my right. We jumped about five or six gates, crossing over from yard to yard.

"I think this good here," Coon said, and went crunched down in between a wooden fence and some bushes.

"Man I don't think we're far enough," I said, and crunched down beside him.

I went in my pockets and pulled out two ounces of weed. I stayed low as I walked to my right a couple of feet and put the two ounces under the house we were behind. I used some leaves to cover it up then went back to our hiding place. As we both were looking through the wooden fence, we saw a cop car passing on South Blvd. The police officer turned into the parking lot by the fence where we were. He got out of his car. We quickly noticed that it was a cop by the name of Long Head, who was known throughout Baton Rouge for his treacherous ways. We stayed down low and quiet as we watched him shine his light all around. Long Head was standing right in front of us, and separated only by a fence and about twelve feet. He was looking toward the other end of the fence. We kept our eyes on him as it looked like he was about to get back in his car and leave. All of a sudden, we didn't make any noise, but he went from shinning the flash light on one end of the fence to shinning it dead in my eyes.

"Don't you fucking move," He said, as he took his gun out its holster.

He started walking towards us, flash light still in my eye right next to where his gun was pointing. I know what the rules of the streets are and I know that we were supposed to bust out running and make him work for his money but we weren't stupid. It's the middle of the night, nobody around, and we're dealing with one of the dirtiest cops in the business. Coon had to be thinking like I was because he didn't move either. When the cop got close enough, both of us stood up and threw our hands in the air.

"You bitches bet not move," He said, then took the walkie talkie from off his shoulders and called for backup. We followed his orders and remained still. A couple more police cars came pulling into the parking lot. They got out and all of them jumped the wooden fence into the backyard where we were. They made us lay down in the grass and handcuffed us both.

"Now how are we gon' get these fuckers back over," The short fat one asked.

"We gon' throw them over," Long Head answered.

They all started laughing, but me and Coon looked at each other, knowing that he's dead serious. The black cop, which was the only black one out the bunch, looked around and seen that we was in someone's backyard. "Come on, we could take them this way," He said, looking in between two houses and seeing a street that was on the other side of two fences. They walked us to the first fence then two of the police officers climbed over it, leaving three officers on the side where we were. One by one the three officers picked us up and hand us over to the other two officers. They got us to the street where four police cars were waiting.

"Is this yours," A tall white cop asked, as he came walking from down the street smiling and holding the SKS in his right hand with the banana clip in the other.

-CHAPTER 17-


The four got off of their first class trip, grabbed their luggage, and walked to the back of the airport to get the two SUV's that awaited them. Jon-Jon had ordered the rentals from Rent-A-Car and told them what time their planes were scheduled to be in. After he paid from over the phone with his credit card, Mr. Ale assured him that his two Denali's would be waiting with the keys in the ignition when they got there; so far so good.

Jon-Jon and Bonnie Shepherd got in one of the trucks while Phat Pat and Lil' Wick jumped in the other one. This wasn't the group's first time visiting Florida. Actually, you could say they were all regulars. Every year they would fly or sometime drive out to Florida at least three times. In March it was Mardi Gras in Daytona, which is what they're doing now. On the Fourth of July they hit up Miami's beaches and in August its right back in Daytona for Spring Bling. This year they had planned on doing it a lil' bigger than the previous years.

Jon-Jon girl, the flight attendant, had told him about Labor

Day Weekend up in Brooklyn, New York. She said it be millions of people on one big long street with all different kinds of floats coming up the middle. When she told him about the Jamaican float that comes through every year with about a hundred-fifty girls dressed like the Jamaican chic from off of the movie Belly it was all he needed to hear. She went on telling him that the girls walk in the street doing those exotic Jamaican dances and you could just go jump behind one of 'em and they'll start dancing on you. The day that Jon-Jon told the rest of the crew about it was the same day that they started the countdown. Lil' Wick plan was to film everything, bring it back, then take two of his flat screen TV's and hang them up on the outside of his house and let the whole hood watch.

They had gotten a room that was on the beach, a suite at the Marriott Hotel. As they road down Beach Blvd they seen that the beach was already packed with people. In Daytona the winter only lasted for three months: December, January, and February. Today the sun showed everybody just what time it was. Which was, time to come up out those long pants and shirts and show off what you go to the gym for.

As they watched all of the pretty faces, bit titties, flat stomachs and long legs, Lil' Wick grabbed his Nextel from off of his lap. "You niggas saw Buffie the Body," He chirped.

"Nigga where you saw Buffie at," Bonnie Shepherd chirped back.

"Y'all ain't seen her?" Lil' Wick repeated.

"Man this nigga high already," Bonnie Shepherd said to Jon-Jon who was sitting on the passenger side while laughing.

"These niggas think I'm bullshitting." Lil' Wick told Phat Pat.

"Nigga you is," Phat Pat responded.

"What!" Lil' Wick said. "Mane, hurry up and take me to the room. I remember what she had on. I'm 'bout to walk up and down this beach and find her."

"Aye, what cha'll boys finna do?" Phat Pat chirped from his line.

"After we come from the room, me and Bonnie gon' shoot down there by Mr. B." Jon-Jon said. "B says he got somethin' sweet for me."

Mr. B is the owner of Diamonds at Volusia Mall. The group always kop's something from Mr. B whenever they come out to Florida.

"I forgot all about B ass," Phat Pat said.

"Well look, Lil' Wick talking about he wanna go chase this Buffie the Body look alike so..."

Lil' Wick cut Phat Pat off before he could continue. "Nah uh mane, don't worry about it. I need to holla at B too.

"Man even if that was Buffie, look around you nigga. They got a thousand Buffies out chea." Jon-Jon said.

"He said he gon' chill," Phat Pat chirped back. "He needs to holla at B his self."

They drove into the Marriott and all of'em jumped out leaving the SUV's running. As two barely legal white boys hurried over to them, Jon-Jon and Phat Pat both left a one hundred dollar tip. The valets showed all thirty-two before signaling for the bellhops to come and get there luggage.

Walking into the hotel, Jon-Jon looked over at the front desk and seen that Terry was working today. Terry is the twenty-three year old red bone with the nice set of silicone titties that usually assist them whenever they stayed at the hotel.

"Hey their Mr. Davis," Terry said, addressing Jon-Jon as he was the first to reach the counter.

"What up wit'cha ma," Jon-Jon responded.

"I'm doing ok." Terry said, while pressing buttons on her keyboard. "How everything been going in Baton Rouge?"

"Everything been good," Jon-Jon leaned over the counter to get a better look at Terry in her bathing suite top.

"Ok," Terry said while looking at her computer screen. She gave Jon-Jon a room key then walked around the counter.

Jon-Jon and Phat Pat walked beside Terry as she started telling them about a new club that just opened on Jeff Avenue call Exquisite. The Shepherds followed behind them while the bellhops went another way with their luggage. Terry continued to control the conversation as they got on the elevator and took it all the way up to the fourth floor, suite 409.

When they made it there, the bellhops were waiting at their door. Terry let them in then introduced to them the big and spacious top of the line Marriot Suite. Equip with two King size beds, a 72"flat screen, and a miniature kitchen that had two bottles of Moet sitting on the counter.

As Terry talked to them about their suite, she walked over to the far end of the room and pressed a button on the wall. The wall separated in half. Jon-Jon them walked over by Terry and looked out of the big glass that the wall opened up to then seen a full view of the beach. They looked at the people walking below for a moment. Terry then led them to a door that had the luxury bathroom behind it.

She walked into the bathroom then went all the way to the other side of it and opened another door. "Her twin," Terry said, while walking into a mirror of the previous room.

"It's on!" Lil' Wick yelled.

"If y'all need anything you could just pick up the phone and dial 9 for room service." Terry handed Jon-Jon the second room key then told them to enjoy as she left out.

Phat Pat went sat on the bed and called up his Jamaican partner. One by one the rest freshened up in the bathroom, brushed their teeth and made sure their diamonds were on bling. Once everyone was good, they all left the room. All four of them jumped in the same truck, leaving the other one behind. The other SUV was the one that Phat Pat had to have to his self being that he always branched off while they were in Florida and did his own thang.

They made it to the mall and all of them stepped in looking like dope boy celebrities. Wearing $1,200.00 Louis

Vuitton glasses, diamonds glowing off of their neck, wrist, ear, and mouth, pants sagging, and swagger on full blast. The four made their way to Diamonds with all eyes on them. Once they reached the store, all of them gave Mr. B some dap. After the greetings, Mr. B led them over to a glass desk sitting in the corner of the store. There were only two chairs sitting in front of the desk that Jon-Jon and Phat Pat sat in. Mr. B asked his young Filipina mixed with black assistant who was standing behind the counter to bring out two more chairs for the Shepherds and to get the gift for Jon-Jon.

Brian and Lil' Wick both declined the chairs and chose to remain standing.

"Are you guys sure," The short, gray-haired, old but very well in shape Mr. B asked.

"Yea we cool B," Brian Shepherd replied.

"Thank you Cyrstal," Mr. B told the assIstant as she came from out of the back and sat a black box in front of him. He then turned the box so that it would face Jon-Jon then slowly opened it.

They all looked in amazement as they watched a medallion that revealed red, blue, white, brown, and black diamonds dancing off of an American flag with the face of a guerilla in the middle of it. The medallion was 24 Carat gold. Mr. B took the piece out as they all seen that it was attached to a chain known as the Miami Cuban Curb link chain. The chain was 14 carat gold with red, blue, and white diamonds in its links. Jon-Jon had called Mr. B and put the order in for the piece two weeks ago. The chain symbolized the initials of A.M.R., as in America'z

Most Rawest. Something that Jon-Jon came up with and been screaming since the age of 13. Mr. B really out did himself with this one. After the rest of the click seen it, they quickly put in an order for the design they wanted.

Jon-Jon followed Mr. B to the cash register then reached in his pocket and pulled out stacks of one hundred dollar bills. He counted out $42,000.

While Jon-Jon was at the register, Phat Pat Nextel started going off. "Yeah," He answered.

"Me outside mon, parked in front of Dillard's." The Jamaican told him.

"Aiight," Phat Pat said. "Give me fifteen minutes and I'ma be around there. You in ya Escalade?"

"Yeah mon."

"Aiight, I'm in a black Denali."

"Ok mon."

After Lil' Wick Shepherd bought an Armani watch, Brian Shepherd bought a Rolex, and Phat Pat got another pair of earrings, they left to meet up with the Jamaican. Everybody gave Phat Pat a grand for the one pound of Florida Keys that he was getting from the Jamaican. That's how much they had planned on smoking within the two and a half days they would be Daytona. The group of four was as thick as thieves, but there was one thing that they didn't trust amongst each other, and that was their getting high supplies. When they got back to the hotel room, they split the pound in four; a quarter a piece.

Their stay in Daytona consisted of everything it was supposed to which was getting high, drunk, and seeing just how big of an orgy they could have. The biggest they got was a group of seven females, all dimes. You see when most women go to these big events outside of their city, like the Mardi Gras Parades or a Mexican Fiesta, their looking to shake up with whoever has a room. Because the Shepherds, Jon-Jon, and Phat Pat wouldn't just anybody, they got to choose from nearly any group of females that they wanted to bring back to the hotel.

-CHAPTER 18-

(Jersey Phat)

"Say Jersey Phat, you serious huh?" My dog Big Whop asked me. I just looked at him crazy then continued with what I was doing. "You breaking a whole key down into dimes and twenties. Do you know how long it'll take you to get off of all that?"

"Listen to me Big Whop. I ain't on that same shit that I used to be with. Nigga I would post up right there in the alley and push this whole brick, rock for rock, before I let somebody come score an ounce, quarter, half or anything from me. Listen to me, in the game, it's all about winning. And you win by staying out chea. Who can last the longest?

Ok so a nigga selling bricks; ten and fifteen at one time. He might last for maybe five years. I'd give the nigga eight at the most before the feds come snatch him up and give him 360 months to life. Nigga he can't enjoy those millions of dollars that he made if he's behind bars. Selling to a hustler is too risky because you'll never know when he got popped. He could've gotten pulled over last night and caught slipping with a whole key in his trunk. They gon' take him in, throw all them big ass numbers in his face and there you have it, another confidential informer. They gon' put him right back out chea the next morning to kop weight from damn near every dope boy in the city, but nah uh not me.

I'ma get my ass out there and sell to cluckers all day long. Cause you know why? Because If they get caught, that's just a paraphernalia charge for them. They gon' do six months in a drug program and be right back out chea. Don't get me wrong, some of those bitches have been known for ratting too, but nowadays what the feds concentrate on is catching a nigga with four and a half or better. You'll never know whether or not a clucker or a hustler is a CI until after you sold them at least four and a half ounces. That could be on the first time, second, or the fifteenth time. The drug game is a risky business no matter which way you look at it so what you should focus on is lowering some of those risks. It's all about who can last the longest my nigga."

-CHAPTER 19-

(Antoine)

After a whole month of being locked up, I had finally gotten some good news. Yesterday I had a visit from my people and my momma told me that the judge dropped the charges on Coon so he'll be back at home any day now. Boy you don't know how good I felt after hearing that. I'm only 15 years old so I'm in Ryan's Detention Center for the juveniles. I know that it's only so much they could do to me but Coon is 19. He went straight to the parish prison. And guess what those dirty ass cops charged us with? Attempted First Degree Murder; ain't that a bitch. Come to find out, Pookie was in the house all along. They're the ones that called the police. The chic that was driving the car must've hurried up and dropped them off then left without me seeing her. Pookie them saw me as soon as I reached the corner with that big ass gun in my hand. Damn I'ma miss my chopper. I didn't even get the chance to have all the fun with it that I wanted to.

Oh and you won't believe what happened the day after we got arrested. As me and my teal was going to second chow, guess who I see walking in this bitch in an orange jumpsuit right along with me? My crazy ass cousin Tito. When I saw him I was like, "what the fuck!" I asked him what happened and he told me that he just couldn't take it. That he was standing in front of the Yang's that morning with Roynell and Lil' Mo when he saw Pookie posted up with all his niggas on the corner by his house. Tito got in the middle of the street and started blasting at the whole crowd.

I'm like, "Huh bruh, that's what's up as long as it wouldn't with my Desert Eagle." He said that it wouldn't and that he went got his partner Devin gun from out the bottom.

Me and Tito had finally gotten on the same teal with each other. At first he was on D Teal and I was on C Teal. Both of us were on the same status as D Teal, which stood for disciplinary teal, but the only reason they didn't put me on that teal is because they was too packed. Tito stayed on good behavior for the whole month so he could move up to C status. The Guards moved him to this teal yesterday.


Once everyone was in from rec, me and Tito kicked off a game of spades with two dudes from Banks Town. On the first hand of the game, we went seven and Banks Town went five. Banks Town to my right dealt so I led out with my ace of spades. Everybody dropped their lowest spade and Tito racked the book. I came back with a four of spade. Four spades dropped again. Banks Town to my left won the book with his king of spade. Banks Town then came back with his ace of club. Tito cut the book with his five of spade. Tito then came back with a seven of spade. This time only three spades dropped. Banks Town to my right was out.

Toward the end of the hand, we had our seven and they needed two more to get their five.  It was my lead so I threw out a jack of heart.  The queen of heart was still in some ones hand, and if Tito had it then they were set because I had the last two spades.  Just like I thought, Tito won the book with the queen.

"Y'all know what time it is, set that five," I said, as I showed the table my last two cards.  "Set they ass," I told the person on the side taking the score.  I threw my cards on the table and reached Tito my fist to give him some dap.  Tito threw his cards on the table then dapped me down.

"Hold up man," Banks Town to my right said, and picked up Tito's cards which were a jack of club and a nine of club.  "Tito you cut clubs."

"Mane I ain't cut no fucking club," Tito said.

"Yes you did nigga.  You cut my partner ace of club out the gate." Banks town said.

"Yea you did cut my shit," Dumb ass Banks Town finally remembered his book being cut.  He went in our books to show where Tito cut his ace of club.

"Fuck!" I said, because Tito cut the book and didn't have to.  We had our books anyway it went.  "Give me the cards."

Everybody pushed their chairs back in and started sliding the cards to me.  As I began shuffling, Tito got up and went to the water fountain.  The water fountain was right behind Banks Town, the one with the big mouth.  When I got finished shuffling, I gave big mouth the cards so he could cut.  Then from out of nowhere, Tito ran on him quick, hitting him with a combination of lefts and rights.  Tito never let up from Banks Town and he never gave him a chance to get out of his seat.  Banks Town just sat there in a ball and took it until one of the guards came and got Tito from off of him.

## -CHAPTER 20-

After the lic, Troy went to his baby momma's house and gave her some money to take care of his eleven year old son with. He never mentioned that he was going out of town and that there was no telling when he'll be back. He then jumped in his Cut-Las, got on Interstate 10, and drove straight to Atlanta, Georgia. With the money Troy had plus the money that Shanice had stashed away, both of them was guaranteed to be straight. Shanice's boyfriend ended up bleeding to death that night. No one found them until two days later. A few of them that wasn't hogtied were able to roll their way to the front door, but with their hands tied behind them and their feet tied together, plus the bottom half of all of their faces smothered in tape, the only thing they were able to do was make a lot of hums and kick on the door in hoped to be rescued. If it wasn't for the mail lady coming on that Monday morning, there's no telling how long they would've been there.

At first, Troy didn't plan on messing with Shanice anymore after the robbery, but when he thought about it then saw just how

blind Shanice had everyone to not suspect that she was setting them up, he knew that he could make some real money with her on his side. Shanice stayed in Baton Rouge until after she went to her boyfriend's funeral then the next day she packed all of her clothes, threw them in her Cadillac, and went out to ATL to meet up with Troy. Troy and Shanice is currently in the process of setting up this big time hustler from outta Columbus, Georgia.

For the past month, Troy has been scoring work from the same person that's spending big on trying to keep Shanice happy. Mr. Columbus think Shanice still lives in Louisiana with her sister, who is the same chic that Shanice was riding in her Range Rover with on the day that Mr. Columbus first stumbled across her. The chic that Shanice was with was actually Troy's sister. Shanice played it like she wasn't interested in him or the Porsche truck that he was driving, but she already knew that she was gonna see just what type of doe Mr. Columbus had rolling in.

She told him that they had come out to ATL for the weekend to go shopping at the underground mall. Shanice gave him her cellphone number which had a Baton Rouge area code of 225 to go along with her lie. Mr. Columbus has been sending her money for a plan ticket out to Columbus every Friday. They've been seeing each other for two months now and Shanice think she finally got him to the point that she need him to be at in order for her to execute her plan which is blinded by love. She and Troy made plans to do him on next Friday. There's just one problem that Shanice have been struggling to cope with. She think that she may have falling in love with Mr. Columbus too.

Carl never was good at selling drugs. He just did it to support his weed habit and to keep a few extra dollars in his pocket. When he was in the tenth grade, he maintained a B average throughout the whole year. Only reason he didn't graduate from Tara High is because his girlfriend at the time had popped up pregnant. At fifteen years old, Carl moved out of his momma's house and went lived with his nineteen year old girlfriend in her one bedroom apartment.

Ms. Deloreious was furious with what Carl was doing to his life. Even though Carl was two feet passed rebellious, two months after the baby was born and six months after he had dun dropped out of school, he decided to listen to his momma and have a blood test taken. His girlfriend was worried to death because she knew that it was a chance that baby Carlos wasn't really Carl's baby.

Come to find out, like on The Morry Show, "you are not the father!" Carl took back everything that he had ever bought for his girlfriend Diane and left her with only the stuff that he bought for the baby then moved back in with his momma. Carl had enough of high school so he refused to go back. He let his momma enroll him in Baton Rouge Community College so he could at least get his GED, which for him was only a four month process. Carl even stayed after he had his GED and majored in computer science for a year.

The money that Carl got from the robbery was enough for him to give up the street life and go back to school to finish his studies.

## -CHAPTER 21-

Jon-Jon mainly sold weight, but every now and then he would break down a couple ounces and get back in the trap. Since he went on that spending spree in Daytona, he decided to grind hard for the next month to get his stacks back looking the way that they were. As he sat on a crate in the cut between 15$^{th}$ Street and Brooks Projects, he saw one of the smokers walking on 15$^{th}$ Street. Jon-Jon whistled three times.

The smoker heard Jon-Jon and excitedly came walking through the cut. "Man I'm glad you back here tonight." The smoker said, after he got through the bushes to Jon-Jon. "I was 'bout to take that walk to Brice Street."

"What's going down wit'chu tonight Leroy," Jon-Jon asked.

"I'm cooling, roune." The smoker replied. "Hook me up with something for sixty."

Jon-Jon work was already sitting on his lap so he opened the plastic bag and pulled out three nice twenties then dropped them in Leroy's hand.

"Nice looking out roune." Leroy balled up his hand with the product inside. "Man it was somethin' that I wanted to talk to you about."

"What's up?" Jon-Jon asked.

"You know that nigga that cha baby momma messing with?"

Jon-Jon knew exactly who he was talking 'bout, "Yea, what about him?"

"Hopefully it's not too late, but chu need to tell her to watch out for that nigga."

"Nigga what the fuck you talking 'bout," Jon-Jon said, getting frustrated by Leroy's prolonging.

"I was on the same line in the parish with him. Man that nigga was fucking them boys in there. Then the boy that he was fucking was deader than a doe nob. Everybody knew he was dead too because the boy used to be in the pill call line every night swallowing 'bout fifteen pills.

## -CHAPTER 22-

(Antoine)

"Kevin Antoine Guillard," The guard called out.

I looked back from one of the movies that us on B status were allow to watch every Tuesday and Friday night, which was the movie The Green Mile, to see the guard standing in the doorway.

"What's up," I asked.

"Come here and see what's up!" The guard responded.

"Bitch ass guard," I mumbled to my roune Mario sitting next to me then got up and walked out the door with the guard. As the door automatically closed behind me, he walked over to the counter and got a white envelope from off the top of it. He gave it to me so I turned around to go back on the teal.

"Nah uh," The guard said. "You gotta read it before you go back in there."

"What!"

"Go sit on the bench," he said.

"Ssshhhh," I went sat on the bench and looked on the front of the envelope. It was a letter from Ebony. I opened it and began reading......

All she was talking about was she miss me and she can't wait for me to come home so she can do this, that, and a whole lot of other freaky bullshit that she been doing ever since I met her. I went took the guard back the letter so I could go back and finish enjoying the movie.

"You don't want to write them back," The guard asked.

I thought for a minute then I told him yeah. He gave me a pen, three sheets of paper, and a stamped envelope.

"Can I get something to write on?" I asked.

He reached below the counter and pulled out the phone book. I grabbed it and went sat back on the bench. No way in hell was I gon' write Ebony back. I thought for a second. Then wrote,

"Trapstar what's up, this ya brother saying what's happening

I'm writing to you, but raping

trying to keep my rhymes trashing

while sitting back and laughing, thinking 'bout the times

we had in that world and what we pulled off to shine

but now a nigga locked up, man that's fucked up

but you know I'ma hold it down I'm 'bout whatever no matter what thug

so if a nigga jump up, you know he'll get his issha

but I ain't gon' lie I'm keeping it real ya lil' brother he miss ya

so this'a, kind of a sad letter

man can you picture, you and me koping Jags together

I know you can cause you the reason I put this 4 in my mouth

and cause of you and the South is why lil' me thugged out

so I count, every day I live up in this hoe

and before I go, so you'll know

you got the first letter I wrote"

-CHAPTER 23-

(Monique)

I only saw Jon-Jon maybe once since Lester been home, and that was when me and Evet was at the store getting a couple pounds of crawfish. While we were in there, he came in talking about he been real busy, like always, so that's why he haven't been around to see his kids. I told him that I didn't live in the projects anymore and gave him the address to my new place. It must have went in one ear and out the other 'cause he never came by and that had to be at least three months ago. He gave me some money that day like that would make up for him not being around. I threw my hands up with Jon-Jon a long time ago in hope that Lester would step up and be that man that J.J and Jonathan needed in their life.

Unexpectedly, Jon-Jon called me earlier and said that he had to talk to me about something important and that he didn't wanna say it over the phone.

I heard a knock on the door and got up from the couch to go answer it. "Hey Stranger," I said, after I opened the door to where Jon-Jon stood.

He walked straight pass me without saying anything, and without me moving to the side to give him the permission to come in.

"Yes, you could come right on in Jon-Jon," I said, still looking outside where he was supposed to be. I turned around to see him walking to the back room with a gun in his hand. "Jon-Jon what the hell is you doing?" I watched him go in and out of each room.

He came back into the living room, "Where that nigga at?"

"Who you talking about; Lester," I asked.

"You know what nigga I'm talking about." Jon-Jon responded in rage, "Where that nigga at?"

"He's gone, why?"

Jon-Jon moved his head from left to right, looking around in the living room. "Fuck."

"Jon-Jon you scaring me, now tell me what the fuck is going on."

J.J and Jonathan came from out of their room. "Y'all go back in the room." I told them. As they were making their way back into the room, Jon-Jon followed behind them. After Jon-Jon returned from closing their door, I told him again to tell me what was going on.

"Monique, sit down," Jon-Jon said.

"No, tell me what the hell is wrong."

Jon-Jon paused for a second, looked me straight in the

eyes, and repeated his self. "Monique, sit down."

I turned around and went sat on the couch so I could hear what he had to say. He came and sat beside me and put the gun on his lap. He put his fist on his mouth and thought for a second. Then he turned and looked at me. I could see him take a deep swallow.

"What's wrong," I asked, in almost a whisper.

"When was the last time you been to the doctor," He asked, with his right hand still covering his mouth.

"When I had Precious, why?"

"Go put some clothes on the baby, I'm 'bout to take you to the hospital." He said, after dropping his hand.

"I'm not going anywhere and why in the hell you wanna take me to the hospital?"

Jon-Jon put his head down then picked it back up. "That bitch ass nigga of yours got AIDS."

"How you know?" I asked, and felt a tear fall down my face.

"'Cause that nigga was fucking them punks in jail," Jon-Jon responded.

I lost control and broke down crying.

"What chu got it," He asked.

"I found out three weeks ago."

"Fuck!" Jon-Jon yelled, as he got up from the couch.

I hurried and grabbed his arm as I stood up with him. "Jon-Jon please don't do him nothing."

"What?"

"Don't do him nothing." I repeated.

"My baby momma is dying and you telling me not to do the nigga nothing."

"That's Precious daddy, and I still wanna be with him."

-CHAPTER 24-

(Antoine)

I had just gotten finished with doing 250 pushups, a light workout, because today was the day that I suppose to go in front of the judge. The guard came and told me earlier after we ate breakfast to be ready by 11:30. He said that I had Judge Brandy. I asked a couple people on my teal if they knew about her and was she cool or what. Two people said that her fine ass was the worst judge to go in front of because she don't cut a nigga no slack.

My dog Lil' Ked from out the Park, who was in the cell next to mine's, told me, "She's cool as long as you cool. If you go in there acting like a big tough man and like you don't give a fuck, she gon' show you that she's tougher and not give a fuck either. If you go in there with your head on your shoulders, saying yes mam and no mam, you gon' come out straight."

"It's that time Guillard," The guard said, then popped open my cell door.

"Good luck thug," Lil' Ked told me, standing at his door as I came out my cell.

"Appreciate it gangsta," I responded, then the guard escorted me off the teal.

When we got in the courtroom, wasn't anybody in there but a tall white cop, a black man in a blue suite sitting at a table, a white man in a brown suite sitting at different table, and a pretty dark skin judge that was reading some papers on her desk. Judge Brandy wore her long jet black hair in a style where all of it was pulled to the back and sticking straight up through a white clip. I don't know why they didn't let me call my people so they could've come.

The guard walked me straight up to the table where the black man was sitting. He stood up and reached his hand out to me. After the handshake, he told me to have a seat.

"How are you doing Mr. Guillard," He asked, as he pulled his chair closer to mine. "My name is Mr. Green and I'll be representing you today." Mr. Green was talking, but it was more like he was whispering to me. "Mr. Guillard, your case is very strange. The officers charged you with attempted first degree murder, but the report is stating that you never shot the gun. How could that be?"

I simply raised my shoulders up and down. "I don't know."

"The guy that you got into it with, Pookie Steevins, was inside the house. Was there anyone outside of the house at the time you were standing on the corner holding the gun?"

I paused and thought for a second. If I answer that question then it'll be like I'm admitting to having the gun. This dude could be trying to set me up. I went ahead and said fuck it to myself and shook my head from left to right, "No."

Mr. Green smiled at me then patted me on the wrist two times.

Aw shit, I think he got me.

"Your Honor, we're ready," Mr. Green said.

"You may Proceed Counselor," The judge responded.

Mr. Green tapped me on the arm so that I would stand with him. "Your Honor, my client has been charged with attempted first degree murder. How can that be possible Your Honor and there wasn't anyone outside at the time. The victims were inside their house and there wasn't any shots fired." Mr. Green said, while slightly laughing at the end.

"Yes, I noticed that." Judge Brandy responded, while looking straight at me. "Mr. Guillard."

"Yes Your Honor," I answered.

"How did you get your hands on an SKS Assault Rifle?"

Damn, another one of those trick questions. I remained silent. I think this is what you would call, pleading the fifth.

"Look at me Mr. Guillard," Judge Brandy said, then took off her eye glasses. "For the last seven years, Monday through Friday, I've seen this at least four times a day. And each time feels the same way as the first. It never lightens up. It literally burns me inside of my heart, every time I see a young, black man, walk into my courtroom. Then, it be for all kinds of stuff. Don't you know Mr. Guillard, that if you ever put your hands on a female and she calls the cops on you then that's domestic violence. If you're ever convicted of domestic violence, a lot of your rights will be taken away from you. You won't be able to vote or you won't be able to voice your opinion on a lot of different matters. I really pray that this young generation will wake up and start to value life. Are you in school? Mr. Green is he in school?"

"Yes Your Honor, he's in the ninth grade at McKinley High School." Mr. Green said while looking down at a piece of paper.

"Make sure that you get your education, Mr. Guillard, and that you stay from out of a courtroom." Judge Brandy said, then looked at the counselor, "Mr. Green, two years of supervised probation."

## -CHAPTER 25-

(Antoine)

You know, it's always fucked up when the hood loses a soldier. I had just got word from Roynell that my supplier Future got robbed and killed three nights ago. Damn, that's a hard pill to swallow. Future was off of $17^{th}$ Street so I had been seeing him around for a long time now. His shine was just starting to come through for him. Must be when he found that connect. Ain't nobody in Baton Rouge have what he had. I'm talking about everything I scored from him was light green and compressed. One hit, guaranteed success.

**-RIP Future-**

..............................................................................................................

Boy, I had just received the news of a life time. Before I got off the phone with Hope, from letting her know that I was home, guess what she told me? She said that she want me to come over, to her house, tonight, while her momma is in the room sleeping. Well, well, well, what do we have here? After eight long months, I'm finally starting to see the entrance door, to heaven. Those two months I did in Ryan's Detention Center must've had her missing a nigga.

"Say Toine, I'm not bullshitting; them bitches was trying to throw them numbers at me," Coon said, as we both stood in front of the Yang's. "Talking 'bout they gon' give me the whole case if I don't tell on you. I knew they couldn't do it, but those bitches drive a hard bargain my nigga." Coon started laughing.

"Yea they were just trying to mess wit'cha head." I told him. "They couldn't do shit but give one of us a pistol charge and I damn sho wouldn't gon' let them give it to you."

"Boy, they told me that if they found my finger prints anywhere on that gun, them bitches was gonna lock me up and throw away the key."

"You knew they were bullshitting then, huh?" I asked.

"I don't know if they were bullshitting, but that's when I started to relax." Coon replied. "I knew for a fact they wouldn't find my finger prints on it 'cause every time I touched that gun I wiped it down. And if you could remember, I never touched it that night in front of Pookie's shit so I was good on that end."

"Look at the ghost out chea," Dirty Red said, riding up on the corner from the side street and getting off of his bike. A bike is what a lot of hustlers used to catch different sells throughout the hood. Dirty Red had two cars. He had a 1979 Monte Carlo and a Delta 88. Me and Coon walked up to him and gave him some dap. "I told ya cousin here that they wouldn't gon' keep you in that bitch for too much longer." Dirty Red said, while looking at me. "Shit, they wouldn't suppose to keep him for no whole month. That wouldn't nothing but a possession of a firearm, y'all first ones. Coon, you should've been out the next day or whenever you went in front of a judge on a $1,500 bond.

On your first time, any bond under 10 G's is a sign out bond.  And then they charged y'all with attempted first degree murder.  Y'all lawyer was supposed to have that shit dismissed from day one. Boy I was out chea going off when I found out 'bout that shit. Coon you wouldn't supposed to stay in there for a month under no circumstances.  Your momma Ms. Trish owns both of those houses right there.  Y'all house and ya grandma house.  Ain't no way in hell."  Dirty Red started laughing.  "Oh and Toine, boy you missed out on some money out chea too."

"Mane I already know I did.  They kept me in that bitch for two whole months like that."  I said.

"Yea fa'real, but don't worry though 'cause I ain't let nothing pass.  I was out chea from morning till night getting it. Boy those two months you been away, changed, my, life."  Dirty Red and Coon both started laughing.

"I ain't tripping, I'ma make it back."  I said, "But look though.  I need you to hook me up wit'cha connect."

"Oh yea, you was scoring from Future, huh?"  Dirty Red continued, "Rest in peace.  How much you were getting from him?"

"I was only getting a half, but I'ma need the whole thang now."  I told him.

Dirty Red looked at the watch on his wrist, "Its 8:30.  You know that's kind of late.  Ain't nothing else gon' come through here tonight like talking about it so if you could wait until the morning, I'd have that for you."

"Yea that's cool."  I responded.  "I could wait till then."

"Alright, because I'm 'bout to go get fresh and fall off in the U," Dirty Red came and dapped us down again. "Y'all Boys ain't going?"

"Not me," Coon answered. "I'm 'bout to go catch up on my rest."

"That's right. I forgot about Mr. Take it in before the street lights come on." Dirty Red said, as he picked up his bike, "Toine you not going?"

"Nah I'm 'bout to go to my girl house in a lil' bit." I answered.

"Time to catch up on some pussy cause I'm desperately needed," Dirty Red was quoting something that Big Head said in one of his songs. "Y'all boys stay up." He yelled, as he paddled away.

"You finna go by Ebony's house gangsta?" Coon asked.

"Fuck no! Nigga I said I'm finna go by my girl house; Hope's house nigga."

"Yea," Coon asked. "That's why you all cheesed up out chea. You finally finna hit."

"After waiting for damn near a year; it's gon' be well worth it though. We probably don't do anything tonight, but this still is a big step. Trust me it's coming."

-CHAPTER 26-

(Antoine)

"Knock, knock, knock, knock, knock."

"Come on!"

"How they gon' come in crazy with the door locked," I
heard Peaches yell to my brother over loud music. She came and
opened his room door.

As I stood at the door, I took a quick survey of Peaches
and made sure she was fully dressed. I did that so that I would
know that my brother wasn't in there naked. Far as long as I
could remember, all of Trap's girlfriends have been light skinned
with big booties. Peaches was no exception.

As Peaches turned around and walked back into the room,
she told me to come on.

I walked in and seen my brother laying on his bed in a gray
tank top, some black Girbauds pants, and the white and gray
Jordan's that came out last week. His favorite rapper was the one
that he had playing on his Play Station, the greatest of all time 2-
Pac. My brother wore his gold rings like 2-Pac. He had tattoos on

his hands, arms, chest, stomach and neck, like 2-Pac; one gold watch and two gold chains with medallions on them. My brother didn't have the ball head. Instead he played a Taper Fade but I'm telling you, he had 2-Pac down pack. It's like he just mixed in a down south swagger with it. He was blowing and shaking on a pair dice in his hands.

"Say Trap, turn that down mane." I said, talking over the music.

The Play Station draw stick was laying next to him on the bed so he picked it up and pressed the pause button.

"Aye mane, I need a favor from you." I said.

"Shoot somethin'," He replied, while continuing to shake the dice.

"Nah mane, I ain't got time for that right now. I need to borrow your car."

"What chu trying to do?" Trap asked, in his slow dragging voice; sounding like he was high. Peaches came from out of the bathroom and lies on the bed beside him.

"Come on mane you already know what I'm trying to do. You know I'm not about to borrow your car to go to the club."

"Awww, he's trying to go see his girlfriend." Peaches said, with both of her hands covering her mouth.

"Girl you better go 'head with all that. I ain't just jumped off the porch." I told Peaches, then looked back at my brother. "But yea, I'm tryin' to go to my girl house."

"Mane I gotta take her home later on," Trap replied.

"I ain't gon' be long at all. She live right there off of Choctaw by Piggly Wiggly." I told him. "Give me an hour and a half, two at the most, and I'll be back."

"Trap stop being mean and let cha lil' brother borrow the car. I ain't gotta be back at the house until 6 in the morning. He's trying to go see his giirrl friend awww." Peaches said.

"Aiight, you could borrow it," Trap said, while throwing me the keys. "But don't be long and ain't no gas in it so you gon' have to fill it up."

"I ain't gon' long at all and I already knew that I had to fill it up."

"You 'bout to go now," Trap asked, then looked at his watch.

"Nah uh, I gotta take a shower first and get geed up." I responded.

"Aiight well look, you ain't gotta worry about rushing back. I'm in for the night so just bring it back before I have to take Peaches home."

"I appreciate it big bro, but I don't need any extra time. After I leave her house, I'm coming straight back over here."

"Aiight, now get out my room."

"I'm already gone," I said, as I closed his room door behind me.

~ 214 ~

-CHAPTER 27-

(Jersey Phat)

It's a Saturday night so me and my dogs are posted at the spot where we always post up at before we go act a ass in Club UPT; right chea on Government Street in the Chop Shop's parking lot. Government Street is one of the main streets in South Baton Rouge. It runs from Goodwood Blvd all the way to downtown by the casinos. The reason we come here is so we could let all of the passing cars check out how a real nigga in the game is supposed to ride.

My dog Big Whop had his, this year's Yukon, parked across from my, this year's Navigator. We haven't too long entered into the new millennium kids, and what we had our whips sitting on, ain't too many mothers fuckers in the world that could say the same; 24's! Come on now. These were special made, special ordered, and a special pick up. All that special shit you already know will require some special stacks.

I passed the blunt of Purple Kush that we were smoking on to my dog Tricky. We chilled there until it was that time. Then the 6 of us, 2 with Big Whop and 2 with me, went jumped in the two SUV's.

We drove down 17$^{th}$ Street then turned right onto North Blvd. North Blvd is a four lane street like Government Street, but it's not as busy. I had been bumping my dog Big Head CD all day so I decided to change it to Soulja Slim. After I put it on track thirteen, I placed both of my hands on top of the steering wheel and turned it all the way to the left then all the way to the right; taking up the whole street. I looked in my rearview mirror and seen Big Whop doing the same thang as we swerved our way to the club.

When we got there, I stopped the SUV in the middle of the street in front of the club. Scooby came and removed the chain. The chain that stood for, parking spots reserved for Jersey Phat and Big Whop/Uptown Superstars! We got out, and all eyes on us. My dog Busta came and `took the lead in front of me. The name Busta stands for, certified head busta. Before we got to the club's entrance, the doorman stopped all of the traffic from going through until we passed. We walked in and around the metal detectors then we went through the second double doors into the club. Being that this is Club Uptown, anywhere we chose to post up at was gonna be an uptown spot. We went to the spot where we were known for being at. I got there and seen all of my other dogs. Dirty Red, Big E, my lil' brother Tavoris, Deno, Danger, Spanky, Crazy, lil'Mo, Big Head, the whole 16$^{th}$, 17$^{th}$, Brice, we in this bitch! I dapped a few of'em down then got in the middle of them. My nigga Tricky came and hand me the bottle of Hennessy. We all act an ass as the D.J put in Big Head's Uptown Superstars. He put it on track #5, one of my favorite songs. The whole club yelled out,

"What, do you see

that got cha hating me,

could it be

I'm from the UPT."

I acted so bad that I started spilling drank on my 1952 Phil Rizzuto #10 throwback exclusive. You know you not finna find this in one of your local stores, huh? And I wasted some on my all white Dope Man G Nikes, not giving a fuck. We stayed there for like thirty minutes then Busta came got my attention for me to follow him. We all went outside to the back of the club where the picture booth was.

Me, Big Whop, Tricky, Big Head, and Dirty Red went stood in the spot where the camera man had a picture of a hand holding four fingers in the air; the symbol of South Side Uptown. Before the camera man snapped, I looked in the crowd and saw my lil' brother standing there with the rest of the south.

"What chu doing over there?" I asked Tavoris. "Nigga you better come get cha ass in this picture."

Tavoris smiled then walked over to us. I grabbed him and wrapped my arm tight around his neck, embraced my lil' brother like brothers are supposed to be. I gave him a kiss on the cheek as the camera man snapped. On the next picture, we got our stunt on fa'real. Everybody pulled out their bankrolls. Me, I pulled out six donkey knots, straight senos.

"Now this how a real nigga in the game live, we get money fa'real! Nigga I got my truck outside sitting on twenty-four inches of nothing but rim. Then the tires are another five inches and two quarters. You know what that mean? Nigga I'm out there riding on thirties. Tell a nigga top that!"

After I got tired of taking pictures, we all took it back in. Big Whop came and gave me the purp. I hit it a couple of times then the whole uptown began punching on this fat nigga that came too close to me. I don't know what the fuck he was thinking. It was the same nigga from Easy Town that we smashed here last weekend. The security guards knew better than to get involved in uptown's business. They stood back and watched as thirty niggas struggled to get a foot in on the nigga's face. I could hear him on the floor screaming over the loud music. I continued to smoke on the purp till his screams came to an abrupt end. The nigga passed out. Busta looked at me and I gave him the green light signal. Three niggas got on one side of the nigga and three niggas got on the other side, as they picked him up and carried him outside through the side door. Later on it'll be six different niggas carrying him in all black. The D.J put it back on Big Head.

"What, do you see,

that got cha hating me,

could it be,

I'm from the UPT."

Twenty minutes later, Dirty Red came and dapped me down. "I'm out my nigga," Dirty Red said over the loud music.

"Already," I asked, after grabbing his hand and pulling him to me so that I could talk into his ear.

"Yea I got something to take care of," He responded back into mines.

"Aiight my nigga, I'ma get at cha on 16$^{th}$." I told Dirty Red, and he turned around and walked off.

Never in a million years would I have thought that I wouldn't be able to keep those last words that I said to him. This was the same night that my childhood homie, Dirty Red, got murdered.

Take a moment and inhale it one time, "Ssshhhwww." Now simultaneously slowly let it blow out through your nose and your mouth.

Come to find out, before Dirty Red went took care of that business, he stopped at Denny's to get something to eat. While he was there, this nigga who was sitting at a table with his bitch, bitch, started eye balling my nigga. Instead of the nigga being a real nigga about the shit and going upside that bitch's head, he went approach Dirty Red. Dirty Red beat the shit out of him, stomped on'em, jumped on'em. Right there in the middle of the restaurant. The nigga couldn't take it so he pulled a gun from outta his pants and hit my homie seven times in the chest. Bitch ass nigga.

**-R.I.P. to the big dog, Dirty Red-**

# -CHAPTER 28-

(Antoine)

It's been two weeks since the death of Dirty Red and my hood still looked fucked up. You know when you got that one nigga that walks into a room and it's like he brings energy to every corner of it then when he leaves he takes out even more than what he put in. Well that's what Dirty Red did to every street corner around here. I ain't gon' lie, the shit looked so terrible that it made me want to take it inside and not come back out until next month. Every car that passed had R.I.P. Dirty Red on the back window and was playing either 2pac's, "Life goes on," or Master P's, "I miss my homie".

The rapper Trina had a concert going on today at the Centroplex that a lot of people went to also, so that's another reason why things looked so dead around here. I would've gone to, but I figured that I'd stay and put in the extra time on the grind. Because Dirty Red died that night, I never got the chance to get that issue from him. I'm working in a different field now. Roynell told me about one of his rounes by the name of Lil' Tim that lived on 13<sup>th</sup> Street. He said that Lil' Tim was the man around there and that he'll hook me up with something nice. I'm glad I listen to him because when we got there, it was obvious that he wouldn't no lil' boy.

Lil' Tim was living in the projects on 13th Street, but when a chic came answered the door wearing a smile and a towel, I knew I wouldn't leave disappointed. Me and Roynell walked in and saw that it wouldn't just him and the chic there, but there were three other girls walking around in some thongs and a dude by the name of Joe sitting on the couch. I knew Joe from seeing him hanging around the projects on 17th Street.

I didn't tell Lil' Tim what I wanted, I just gave him a thousand dollars and told him to hook me up with something. Boy, what he hooked me up with made me realized that I been bullshitting with the other stuff. Whatever that was that he gave me, I broke down into $3,100 worth. With that kind of profit, that means that I'm tripling my money plus putting an extra hundred on top of it. Aye, Lil' Tim show love.


I never told you what happened with me and Hope that night at her place, huh? I bet you would like to know. Come on nah, you know I can't tell you something like that. That's a bond that should be kept sacred. It should be concealed, not revealed. Enclosed, not exposed. Entrapped, not.... Hold up a minute.

"Hello."

"Hey Toine," Hope said.

"What's up my Boo Bear, what chu doing over there?" I asked. From the number that popped up on my cell phone, I knew that she was calling me from her house.

"Me and Leo just came back from the concert," Hope answered.

"So how everything went, did you have fun?"

"Yea, it was nice, but I wish you would've come with us."

"You know I would've came with cha'll ma, but I had business to take care of."

"Huh uhm muh hum huh," Hope made that moping and complaining noise because she hated whenever I told her that I had business to handle.

"There you go with all that again," I said. "Trina gon' be back. We'll check her out next time together."

"You not gon' believe what happened to y'all dog from around there?"

"Who you talking about?"

"That boy with all the money that be over there," Hope said. "What's his name, Jersey Phat."

"Oh Lil' Ivy, what happened?" I asked.

"He was on stage with Trina."

"Yea?"

"Uh huh."

"Well I ain't surprised," I said. "What chu expect, Jersey Phat is from Uptown."

"Whatever," Hope said. Mad 'cause it wouldn't none of her bottom boys.

While I was sitting on the wooden box in front of the Yang's, Twin and Crazy came walking up from the side street, Bynum Street.

During those two months that I did in Ryan's, my momma found out about a G.E.D. school that was opening up by where we lived. Being that I would be two months behind in all my classes, she decided to enroll me into the G.E.D School. The name of the school was called The Rennissance Youth Build Program. The school pays the students an allowance of $280.00 every two weeks just for coming. While you're there, you pick up a trade in carpentry and all. When she told me about it, my only response was, "O.K momma, good idea."

I continued my conversation. "So what was you telling me about that dance you got coming up?"

"It's the ninth grade ball," Hope said. "And you better be there."

"Don't worry, I'm coming," I reassured her.

"Fa'real Toine," Hope spoke in her whining voice. "This is important to me. And it's not like we're gonna stay there the whole time."

Hope lost me with that last comment. "Come again?"

"I said we're not staying there. I want you to take me to the place."

I remained silent.

~ 223 ~

"I want, for you, Antoine, to take me to the hotel."

"Yea?" I asked, showing my excitement.

"Uh huh," Hope answered, while laughing.

"You sho' huh," I asked.

"I'm positive," She answered.

"Well it sound like you got your mind made up to me."

"So you gonna come?"

I paused and thought for a second. "Hold up a minute. You ain't gotta tell me that just to get me to come. I'm coming regardless. You my girl so if you wanna go then you not going by yourself and for damn sho' you not going with another nigga. We're going. And we don't have to go to a hotel room afterwards, if you not 100 percent sure you're ready then we're not going to one. We could wait another 8 months or we could wait until you turn 18. We gon' still be together and I'ma still love you more and more each day."

"You see, that's why I love you so much." Hope said. "I know I'm ready."

"This nigga over here making love on the phone," Crazy yelled, ease dropping on my conversation. "Twin, you should've heard what he just said; Toine boy you vicious. 'Baby I love you more and more each day.' Nigga that gotta be Hope that you on the phone with."

"Who else it's gon' be," I asked. "Say, get away from me anyway; listening to a nigga on the phone."

"Say, check that bitch out." Twin said, looking at a maybach coming up the street.

I stood up as well and wondered who the hell it was. Didn't nobody around here have a maybach. As the Mercedes Benz came driving slowly up 16$^{th}$, it pulled right up in front of us and stopped.

Twin was only about two feet away from it as all of us tried to get a good look at the driver. I was on the right of twin, about two feet away, and Crazy was on twin's left. The driver, a black man wearing a suit and tie, kept his head forward. All of a sudden, the curtains to the back window came opened. What twin focused his eyes in on had him frozen. The Mercedes Benz Maybach then slowly drove off.

"Twin stayed in the same spot, only moving his head, as he looked at me then at Crazy. "What the fuck," he asked.

"Mane I know I ain't just see what I think I seen." Crazy said.

"Twin that was your brother, huh," I asked, the only one not getting a good look in the back seat.

Twin looked me straight in the eyes with a look that was mixed with seriousness and a smile. "Jersey Phat, was in the back seat, getting head, from the Baddest Bitch, Trina."

# -CHAPTER 29-

(Antoine)

Later on that night while I was still on 16<sup>th</sup>, Ebony popped up on the block in the car with some white chic and ask me to come go with her. At first I wasn't gon' get in. I told her that I was on the grind and I'll holla back at her some other time. That's when she got out and pleaded with me, whined and begged of course, so I went ahead and jumped in the car to see what she had to say.

Since I been home, I haven't been rocking with Ebony at all. She's always calling my phone, and whenever I do answer, I'd brush her off in less than a minute by telling her that I'ma call her back and never do. It's been almost a month now and tonight is my first time actually seeing her. Since I don't go to McKinley High anymore, I'm not guaranteed to be over here throughout the week. And whenever I come on the weekend, I'm always spending the night by Monique's house. Monique told me that she can't even remember when was the last time that she saw that lame ass boyfriend of hers and since it's not likely of him being around or any other man for that matter, how she put it, I could spend the night there whenever I wanted to. She gave me a key to her house and all.

When I got in the car with Ebony and her girl, I quickly saw that it was exactly like I had thought. Ebony didn't want a damn thing. All she wanted was to be around a boss nigga. Her friend, the driver, was looking right though. Rachel had big titties and she was thick for a white girl. I had to give one of my niggas the opportunity to smash.

When I left the house this morning, to jump on the city bus and come over here, Trap was still knocked out in his room with Peaches. Me and my brother have a lot of similar ways when it comes to females. Neither one of us can be around the same one for too long. I knew that if he was at the crib then nine times out of ten Peaches wouldn't be there.

We picked Trap up about thirty minutes ago. He wanted to get some drank so we went half on a gallon of Taaka Vodka. We got four ice cups and some cranberry juice for the girls. Me and my brother are known as uncut soldiers. We don't mix our alcohol with nothin'.

Me and Ebony was in the back seat and Trap was sitting in the front with Rachel. We all were pretty buzzed, laughing and tripping over really nothing. That's when I felt Ebony's hands unzipping my pants. She pulled it out and began stroking it. Rachel must have noticed the sudden quietness coming from the back so she turned around to see Ebony's head going up and down on my lap.

"I can't believe this," Rachel said, while looking back and smiling. "Boy your brother is in the back seat getting head."

After Ebony got her pleasure out of going down on me, she pulled back and started taking off her pants. She took'em off then got on top of me backwards and held on to the front seat where Trap was sitting as she began bouncing up and down.

"They fucking in the back seat," Rachel said.

I guess Trap said that he had to do something. He pulled Rachel's right titty out of the top of the spaghetti strap shirt she was wearing and started sucking it as she drove. I watched Rachel as she put her right hand on the back of my brother's head while moaning to let him know that he was doing a good job.

"Girl you gotta hurry up and get us to the house." Ebony said.

"Shit, what you think I ain't trying to hurry up and get there?" Rachel asked. "I'm driving as fast as I could. Oooh ooh, suck that titty boy."

# -CHAPTER 30-

(Antoine)

I swear this gotta be me at my best. Black tuxedo, white boutonniere pinned on the jacket, black Stacy Adams, gold tie sitting on a white dress shirt, gold handkerchief sticking out the top jacket pocket, and the compliments comes from the diamond cufflinks; too too sharp. My hair is braded to the back in the fresh Allen Iverson style, Steve Harvey lining, diamond studs in both ears, and the four slugs in my mouth are polished and shinning extra hard. More important than all of that player made shit I just named, the sickest thing of the night is no doubt the corsage in my hand, perfect gentleman.

I parked the Cutlass Ciara in the student parking lot, jumped out, hit the alarm, and proceeded to gangster walk to the school's auditorium. Before I left the house, my brother hit me up with some of his Ralph Loren Polo Cologne then gave me his gold nugget watch to rock, dapped me down, and told me to pick up some tic tacks on the way. My momma, she couldn't even put her digital camera down long enough to give me a good hug. I know for a fact that she snapped over 30 films. You should have seen her in there; she was like a mad woman. She took pictures of me in the house, walking out the house, and getting in my brother's car. I think I seen her in the rearview mirror standing in the doorway snapping as I drove off. That's my moms.

When I made it to the back of the school, where the gym was, I seen some of the students standing against the wall. I nodded my head at them and walked through the open doors. I got all the way in then stopped to look around at everybody. Some of the students were dancing and some was standing on the side. As I continued to look, I turned my body to go left, but when I looked to my right, my sight paralyzed me. Hope was coming to me in an all gold shinning dress. The dress wasn't fitting her tight nor was it too loose. It was spaghetti strapped and hanging down to her caves. The dress was just right. Everything about her tonight was just right. Her gold pumps with the hole in the front that showed off her perfect pedicure toe nails which was complimented by a gold bracelet that she wore on her left ankle, the diamond wrist band and the gold necklaces with an emblem of the cross on it. Everything about her tonight was perfect.

I started walking to her slowly while tryna hold on to every moment. The closer we got, the more I couldn't help but wonder if I was in a dream. From the bounce in her curls, to the swing of her hips, to the sparkle in her eyes; everything about this scene was that of a fantasy. At that moment, I knew what I found in Hope was something special, unique, and rare. What I found in me was something strange, something that I never knew of, something that......... I'm in love. Aye, I'm really in love. I never want to be with another woman again in my life. I don't ever want to see another woman again. All I want is her. We reached each other and embraced in a tight and warm hug. We had to be having some of the same thoughts because she didn't wanna let go of me no more than I did of her.

"You my trophy," I whispered in her ear, and felt her squeeze tighter.

We both were oblivious of anyone around us. At that moment, all we knew was each other and the feelings we were experiencing. When she went back, her hands still tied around my neck and my arms secured around her waist, I looked into her face and saw that her eyes were watery and the bottom of'em was wet.

She formed her mouth to say, "I love you," and I returned her gift with a, "I love you too ma."

We released each other and I put my right hand in my pants pocket to pull out the white handkerchief I had. I gave it to her then I began to open the corsage box that I held in my left hand. I took it out and put the box in my jacket pocket. The corsage was white with gold trimmings on it. I grabbed her left hand and slid the corsage onto her wrist, the opposite wrist of the one with the diamond bracelet. The song Usher and Monica's, "Slow jam," came on. I took the box out of my pocket and was about to go put it on the table that had the refreshments on it, until I seen Hope's best friend Melanie coming over to us.

"Hey Antoine," Melanie said, and took the box from me. "I got this."

"Thank you Melanie," I said, before she walked off.

"May I have this dance," I asked, showing her the gentleman side of me, which is the second stranger that I found tonight.

Hope smiled and said, "Always."

She put her arms back around my neck as we slow danced. I remembered when I saw my cousin Big Luck slow dancing with his girl Tameka at this party they had at the YMCA. Me and Zeus thought it was corny so we were on the side line laughing at him. That was last year sometime, but I still remembered everything he did. Tonight it came in handy as I put both of my hands on Hope's ass while pulling her closer to me to make sure that we didn't let any air come between us.

My mind couldn't help but regress and regret ever getting involved with Ebony. I can't believe that I cheated on my girl. There's no girl in this world worth it and especially not Ebony. Fuck Antoine! One day I'ma have to come clean and tell Hope. I just hope that she'll be able to forgive me and still stay with my crazy ass.

After "Slow Jam" went off, the D.J put in Brian Mcknight's, "Only one for me". The song played halfway through then Hope took her head off of my chest, gave me a kiss, and asked if I was ready.

"When you is," I told her.

"Come on," Hope said, and grabbed my hand.

We walked to the side by the bleachers then Hope turned around and began scanning the dance floor. When Melanie saw me and Hope standing on the side, I could see her telling her dance partner to come with her. They made it over and Melanie introduced us to her friend. I said what's up to Jacob as we dapped each other down. Jacob looked kind of older than us so just like me I knew he didn't go to school here either. Me and Jacob followed Hope and Melanie down to the end of the bleachers where Melanie opened up a black jacket that was sitting on the first row. She hands Hope a gold purse then me the box that I gave her on the dance floor. Hope then pulled me by the hand.

As we walked off from them, Melanie said, "Bye Toine and y'all be good."

"It will be," I said, but only loud enough for Hope to hear.

"She laughed as we continued to walk out the gym. When we got to the car, I deactivated the alarm and walked Hope on her side so I could get the door for my lady.

"Thank you," she said, smiling as she got in and made herself comfortable on the brown leather seats.

After I closed her door, I opened the door in the back, took off my jacket and laid it on the seat. I walked around the car, loosened the tie, unfastened the top two buttons on the shirt, pulled the shirt from out of my pants then unloosened the belt. "Much better," I said, as I opened the door and got in.


I had already gotten the hotel room before I came to the dance. I knew that I had to have her back at the school before her daddy came to pick her up for 10:30, so I got a room that was only 15 minutes away from the school; downtown at the Holiday

Inn. Every time my brother gave me the car he would always give me his driver's license with it. Somebody could easily mistake me and Trap for twins, and they have on a lot of occasions. Whenever he didn't feel like cashing his checks, he would tell me to go cash it for him. Being that you had to be at least 18 to get a room, I got the room using his I.D.

I held Hope's hand as I drove.

"You see, if you would have stopped being scared and met my parents, you could've come and pick me up from the house," Hope said.

"I want to meet your momma and daddy, I mean, your momma sound real nice over the phone but,"

"But nothing Antoine, she is nice. She not gon' trip about your gold teeth. I'd see if you had a mouth full or if you had them all in the front, but yours look cute. She'll like em." Hope said.

"You sho'," I asked.

"I know she is," Hope responded.

"Aiight then I'ma meet'em when I take you home tonight."

"Who you taking home," Hope asked, while looking at me crazy, but still cute. "You must be trying to get killed."

"Look woman, I ain't worried about your dad. I know he's an OG and all. My uncle told me who your daddy was and how he used to get down with the South Side Recking Crew, but he not gon' do me nothing. All I have to do is mention my last name

~ 234 ~

to him and he gon' shake my hand then welcome me into the family."

"Yea," Hope asked.

"Yea," I answered.

"Well you try taking me home then and we'll see just how it goes down." Hope said.

"Nah I'ma chill for tonight."

"Oh alright."

"Say don't say it like that 'cause ya daddy not spooking nothing. I'ma chill tonight on the strength of you. I don't want chu to catch a whooping." I said, turning around to back up into the parking spot at the hotel while still holding her hand.

"You sure that's the only reason," Hope asked, as I put the car in park.

"I ain't scare of your daddy ma." I said while looking her in the eyes.

"I bet chu not."

"Come here," I said, and leaned toward her. We gave each other a passionate kiss. When it ended, I asked, "You ready."

She shook her head up and down, never breaking the eye contact.

"You bet not touch that door." I told her, and pulled the key from the ignition, got out, then went around and open it for her. I grabbed her hand and helped her get out.

I told the lady that work's here in the office that I needed a room on the first floor so we wouldn't have to deal with any steps. Being that we're so close to the casinos, this hotel usually is booked. I guess we got lucky. I parked the car right in front of our room door. While I was here, I came in the room and turned off the AC that the hotel keeps on full blast. We walked in and the temperature of the room was perfect. Hope looked around and saw the ice bucket sitting on the dresser in between the two beds with two bottles of Smirnoff in it. As we stood with my arm wrapped around her, I guided her around the first bed.

"Why you got two beds," She asked.

"This was all they had left on this floor."

We sat down on the first bed with her being the closest to the dresser. She grabbed one of the Smirnoff and hand it to me. I took the top off for her then got a sip out of it before I hand it back. She drunk a lil' bit then said, "This is good." She took another swallow then came in to shower me with kisses. I got the bottle out of her hand and sat it on the dresser then placed both of my hands on her waist and put her on top of me. We remained kissing as she took the tie off of me and started unbuttoning my shirt. Her dress was already up to her waist so I started pulling it up more.

"Hold up a minute," She said, and got up from me.

I watched her as she went into the bathroom. I started coming out my clothes and laid them on the other bed. I still had my size on me that I came home from Ryan's with. Matter of fact, before I got dressed tonight, I did 500 pushups just to make sho' I was right. I took off all of my clothes but the fresh pair boxers then I sat on the bed and waited. When Hope came out of the bathroom, I was stoned. I couldn't move, blink, or do anything but stare. The light in the room was off, but she left the bathroom light on with the door open. Hope had on a white bra, the kind that only goes around a female's body and didn't have the straps, which had her B-cups looking righter than ever, and she wore a pair of matching white thongs to go with it. Her caramel skin was fully lotion and looked softer than soft, thick thighs, skinny waist, flat stomach, and gorgeous face. After she gave me a beautiful pose in front of a big mirror on the wall, she came got back on top of me. We kissed as I fell back.

I didn't really smoke cigarettes anymore, but every blue moon I would buy a pack of Kool and have them until they went stale. As me and Hope sat in the student parking lot, I had all four windows rolled down with my left arm hanging out as I made sho' that I didn't get any smoke on her. The time was 10:15 pm. Her dad should be pulling up soon, but she said that she wanted to wait a minute before she got out.

"You gon' stay at the room tonight," Hope asked.

I took another hit of the Kool then threw it away after I looked at it and saw that it was at the halfway point. I didn't bother to put all of those clothes back on. I just put on the shoes, pants, and the tank top.

"Yea I'ma go chill back over there," I responded. "I got it until checkout time at noon tomorrow so I figured I'd stay and work on some of my rhymes. Aye but look, I wanted to ask you if you needed some money."

"You gon' give me some money," Hope asked, excitedly.

"Why you asked me like that," I asked.

"'Cause you never gave me any money before," Hope said.

"'Cause you never asked me," right after I said that, that's when I realized. "Daammn, all this time I been tripping. I'm sorry ma."

"Yes you have been tripping." Hope said.

"Say, you gotta realize something. This is the first real relationship that I ever been in. I didn't know that I'm supposed to give you money. I mean, if you would've asked me then I would have given it to you with no problems. But I never thought that I'm supposed to automatically do it without chu asking. I need you to do me a favor." I said, while going into my left pocket. "If you ever see me not doing something that you know I'm supposed to be doing as your man," I peeled off 5 twenty dollar bills and gave it to her. The smile that came across her face was like Christmas. "I want you to know that I'm not doing it intentionally, so I need you to let me know."

Hope quickly came in to give me a hug and a long wet kiss.

"Girl you gon' have this smoke all on you," I told her.

"So, I love you," Hope responded.

"I love you too ma. You gon' do that for me," I asked.

"I got chu."

"Your daddy should be pulling up soon."

"Yea I know," Hope responded, and pulled the nob on the door. She pushed it halfway opened then turned to look at me one more time before we departed.

"Come here," I said, then kissed her again. "Call me when you make it to the house."

"I will," She said, then got out, closed the door back, and limped toward the building.

"You need me to help you to the school," I yelled out the window, while laughing.

"I got it!"

-CHAPTER 31-

(Antoine)

It's been over a month since the dance and things with me and Hope have been going excellent, same as before. I still have been kicking off lil' arguments with her every now and then just to see her pout for a few seconds, but they wouldn't bout nothin'.

Back at the crib in my room, I had been on the house phone with Hope for over three hours now. And for the last fifteen minutes, my cell phone has been blowing up from no greater disappointment other than Ebony. I haven't talked to Ebony since the last time when me, her, my brother and Rachel was together, and I messed up and had sex with her. That morning when I opened my eyes and saw that I was in an unfamiliar place then noticed that I was laying on the floor with Ebony beside me, I could've pulled out one of the plats in my head. I jumped up, woke Ebony ass up, then went in Rachel's room and woke up her and my brother's butt naked ass and told Rachel that she had to take us home A.SAP. I told Ebony then that I didn't wanna have any more dealings with her. Before they took us home, I had Rachel to stop by Ebony's grandma house so I could get all of my stuff from over there.

That was over two months ago. Now all of a sudden she wanna start back calling me. After she called the second time, I had to hurry up and put the phone on vibrate. That was still too late. I guess two times really is too many because Hope asked me who that was calling me at this time of the night. I told her that it was somebody calling from an unknown number and I don't answer those calls.

"Who could be calling you this late from an unknown number?" Hope asked, with her mind in prowling mode.

"Shit, your guess would be just as good as mine."

When my cellphone stopped vibrating and the line beeped, I looked on the caller ID box that I had stuck to the wall and saw that it was Ebony. I knew answering it would be like throwing gasoline on a small fire. Have you ever heard the saying, "Curiosity killed the cat"? Well if that's true then I guess that I'm long gone because I had to see what the hell she wanted.

"Aye, hold up a minute Hope."

"Uh huh," Hope responded, before I clicked over

"Ebony why in the hell are you calling me? You know we don't get down no moe."

"Toine, I'm pregnant."

Felt like all systems shut down in my body when I heard those words. "Stop all that lying," I said, after I gained my composer back.

"You wanna see the test for yaself?" Ebony asked.

"Even if you are, you better go run that shit on one of those other niggas." I told her.

"What other niggas? There was never anybody but..."

"Aye look, miss me with this shit." I said, and put the phone back on the receiver. It rung once to let me know that I forgot about Hope on the other line. "Shit," I picked the phone back up and put it to my ear. "Hello," I said. Hope started laughing, so I said it again. "Hello."

"Uh huh," She finally responded.

Why every time you put a person on hold to them seconds feel like minutes and minutes feel like hours? I held the phone and waited for it.

"So you not gon' tell me who that was?" Hope asked.

"What," I played like I didn't hear her.

"When you clicked over, who was that on the other line?"

"Aye man, go 'head with all that?"

"I just wanna know who you were on the phone with for all that time."

"Say Hope, fa'real man, chill out with that shit."

She laughed for a second then came back with, "So you're not gonna answer me?"

"Say look, it's kind of late; you must be tired so I'ma just hit you back tomorrow."

"Uh huh whatever," Hope said, and hung up the phone.

I went laid on the patty that I had made and thought about that call from Ebony. That girl gotta be lying. Ok, I didn't use a condom that night, but I know I ain't trip out and bust in her. Damn that Taaka Vodka. Ebony gotta be lying though. She gotta be. She just trying to trap a nigga with that shit, and that's something that she'll never be able to do with me.

I thought about calling Hope back and apologizing for the way I just talked to her, but then I looked at my digital clock that I kept on the floor not too far from where I laid at and saw that it was 12:19. I decided against it. I had to wake up early in the morning so I could be at school for 7:00. Even though it's the summer time and all the rest of the schools were out, Renaissance Youth Build was a 16 month program that only closes for the Christmas Holidays. However, tomorrow is Payday Friday, one of my best times of the week. Throughout the week, I do a lot of extra things with most of the students in the class. It's mainly gambling, but I be breaking they ass. Tomorrow, other than my check for $280.00 that I get from the school, I gotta pick up a total of $320.00 from five of the students.

"I'll call my baby and make it up to her tomorrow." I told myself then closed my eyes.

-CHAPTER 32-

(Antoine)

The Renaissance Youth Build is a program that only allowed 28 handpicked students to attend. The requirements are, you have to be in the age rank of 16 to 25, you have to come at the beginning during enrollment time, and they have to feel like you would be a success to the program. I made my 16<sup>th</sup> birthday right at the time of the enrollment period. After I went in front of the two consolers, Mr. Pears and Mr. Wallace, they said that they wouldn't gon' pick me at first. I guess those discriminating bastards didn't like the way my pants sagged. But then they told me that it was something I said that made them change their minds. They never did tell me what that something was and I never cared to ask once they told me I was in.

After school ended and everyone had their checks, me and my roune Heat jumped in the car with our roune Stan. The three of us always road together on paydays and went cashed our checks at the Capitol One Bank on Government Street. The three of us riding together was a good thing for me because Heat was always the one who owed me the most out of all the students. Not saying that Heat would play games with me. I never ran into that problem before. I guess it just feels good to keep your eyes on the prize.

When we got to the bank, we saw a couple of the students' cars parked outside. Stan parked then the three of us got out and went in. Two of the students that was walking out the bank past by me and made their drop offs.

"Aiight, you boys be cool." I told them, and went stood in the line.

All of the payments went as plan. I had no doubts that it wouldn't though. Me and Stan cashed our checks before Heat so we waited outside by the car for him. When he came out, he came to me and slapped a stack of twenties, tens, and fives in my hand, payment of $180.00.

"Mane, I ain't fucking with chu no moe," Heat complained. "I can't keep doing this shit to myself. I go to school every day so I can have my checks looking right."

Me and Stan were cracking up listening to Heat kick his self in the ass. "Your check was looking right, huh?" I asked.

"It's looking right for you," He answered. "Fuck, you got more of my check than I do."

"Say Heat, what chu finna do?" Stan asked.

"I'm 'bout to go jump in the car with Keisha them," Heat answered, while dapping Stan down. "This the last time," Heat told me, as we dapped each other down too.

"Man, stop all that tripping over nothing." I told him, before he walked off toward Keisha's car.

"We gon' fuck wit'cha Heat," Stan yelled, then opened his car door.

I went around and got on the passenger side.

"Say roune, you feel like going to the south?" Stan asked, while starting up the car.

"Yea that's cool," I answered. "Why what's up?"

"I gotta go down in the bottom and pick up this bread that my cousin owes me. I was gon' drop you off on 16$^{th}$ then swing back through and get chu on my way out." Stan is originally from the south too, but he been living with his people in Fair Field for the last few years.

"Yea that's what's up," I responded. "I need to go over there and make some moe money anyway."

"Cool," Stan said, then lit the Kool cigarette that he had dangling from his lips.

When Stan turned on 16$^{th}$, we seen the Yang Gang posted up.

"You want me to drop you off down there," Stan asked, looking at the crew of hustlers.

"Yea," I answered.

"Aiight Toine," Stan said, stopping in the middle of the

street, in front of the Yang's. "Give me about thirty minutes."

"Aiight," I responded. "You gon' see me out chea," I got out and closed the door behind me.

"Toine, boy it been rolling out chea." Crazy quickly informed me.

"I figured it was," I said. "That's why I came out chea. Ain't none of y'all seen Doc?"

"Nah uh, that nigga still at work," Coon answered. "Why, he owes you too?"

"Yea, but I ain't gon' get that until next week on the first." I said.

"How much chu got him in the hole for Toine?" Crazy asked.

Usually I don't feel comfortable discussing my business in front of all these niggas, but most of them was my family anyway. "He owe me a bill."

"Oh, you ain't got nothin' to worry about." Crazy said. "He gon' pay on time, I can vouch for that. I used to 2 for 1 him all the time. Those first of the month checks come like clockwork."

"Say Toine, what's up with you and Pookie?" Roynell asked, "Y'all still beefing?"

"I'm not 'bout to keep fucking with that boy and lettin' him mess up my money." I said.

"Straight up," Crazy said. "Fuck that nigga. When my

nigga Tito come home anyway?"

"The last I heard was that the judge was supposed to give him six months," I answered.

"Damn, that's fucked up." Crazy stated.

"Shit, that's good," Roynell told him. "Tito was on papers until he turn twenty-one.

About time I noticed the blue Malibu in the street, it was too late for me to move. "Shit," I said, as Rachel stopped the car in front of us and Ebony jumped out.

"Toine, I need to talk to you," Ebony said, after she walked up to me.

"Say mane, go 'head on with all that." I told her while taking a couple steps back.

"Toine, The doctor appointment is Monday and I want..." Ebony said.

"Say mane, go 'head on." I said, sensing myself about to do something that I would later regret.

"Toine, I'm having your baby and you not gon' come?"

"Bitch, I said get the fuck on," I started walking towards her.

She turned around and walked to the open car door while nodding her head up and down and mumbling to herself. They drove off. I was so mad, pissed off, and embarrassed that I didn't even wanna look at the niggas around me. Everybody went to talking at the same time. I told Roynell, who was the closest to me, "That bitch ain't pregnant for me."

Stan pulled up in front of the Yang's just in time. I walked to his car without saying anything to anybody.

"Aiight Toine," Roynell yelled.

While Stan was on his way to my house, I ran it down to him what happened. Stan was 23 years old so I was looking for some advice from someone older than me and probable would be familiar with this type of stuff. But all Stan did was shook his head and told me to have a test taken. He told me that if we took a test and the baby came out to be mine then she could put me on child support.

"I'm not tripping about no child support because if it's mine then I'ma take care of it anyway, but that bitch ain't pregnant for me. I got a whole ole lady. I can't have Ebony going around telling people this shit.

Stan continued to shake his head. "Damn my boy."

When we pulled into the parking lot, he said, "Just go in there and try to come up with a game plan."

Aiight my nigga," I said and dapped him down. I grabbed my book sack from off the back seat.

"I'ma get at chu Monday." Stan said, as I got out the car.

"Aiight my nigga," I responded, while closing the door.

The situation had me so drained that I couldn't even lift

my arm to put my book sack on my back. I let it drag on the ground as I slumped my way up the stairs.

After walking up the steps, I dust the dirt from off of the book sack then finally threw it over my shoulders. Right before I made it to the door, I looked out into the parking lot and saw my auntie Trish pulling in with Monique on the passenger side and somebody else in the back seat. I couldn't make out who was the person in the back seat. Seeing them coming to our place was kind of odd because from my understanding they had never been there before. I continued going into the apartment, but I left the door opened for them to come in. As soon as I got inside, the pastor's deacon came up to me holding his arms out like he was stopping me from walking any further while telling me to go upstairs.

"For what," I questioned.

"Just go upstairs Antoine," He repeated.

I ran upstairs to Lashey's room so I could find out what was going on. When I got in her room, she was sitting on the bed with her arms wrapped around her stomach while rocking back and forth and crying uncontrollably. I saw my lil' brother pacing in a small spot with his fist balled up.

"What the hell is y'all problem?" I asked them.

"Mane Pastor Franklin been down there beating on momma," Jamain answered.

"Fuck!" I said, then hurried up and ran to my closet. I ran back out and took the steps four at a time. The deacon saw me coming and ran out the front door. I opened the door to my momma's room then went in and saw the pastor standing over her with his fist balled up and threatening to hit her again. He looked my way when he heard the door open. My momma hurried and got off the floor.

"Antoine I'm leaving him. Don't worry about it, we leaving." My momma said, while fast walking over. When I looked into her face, I couldn't find any bruises. I had heard about those people who knew exactly how to hit someone without leaving any marks then I thought about his Marshal Arts skills.

"Boy what chu doing in my room?"

While my momma was now in my left arm, I looked at the pastor and pulled my other arm from behind my back; the arm holding the Desert Eagle, and "Blahhhhh."

-CHAPTER 33-

Lester found himself living in the Alamo Inn, which is a cheap motel where mostly crack heads and prostitutes lived, feeling like he was on his last leg. He finally found a way to combined all of his drug habits into one.

Lester knew exactly what he did to Monique and he knew that by now, she knew. The memories of what he did while he was in jail, those nights when he chose to get high, had been haunting him every night for the past two months. When he first came home, he was in denial that there was a chance of him being infected with the virus. Lester no longer fought that denial faze.

At the Alamo Inn, where he and a smoking drag queen now were, Lester had been playing a serious game with himself. He had lost at the game twice. And every time he lost, he would put a twenty piece into a glass pipe, light it, and suck on the pipe until the substance would disappear. He had a bottle of E&J that he's been using to take him to that high of feeling incredible. The transvestite prostitute was laid across the bed so high that he was unaware of if he was going to sleep or dying.

After Lester hit the bottle again, he pulled the chamber out of the .357 revolver, saw the shinning gold bullet, spent the chamber around real good and popped it back in. Lester was tired of losing at the game so after he cocked the gun, he put the barrel into his mouth and, "Blahhhhh."

He finally won.

# -CHAPTER 34-

(Antoine)

Not even six months had past and I was right back in Judge Brandy's courtroom. I just knew she was gon' let me have it this time.

"Court in session," said the same bailiff as before.


Come to find out, I came out good. The judge only gave me a year in boot camp. I didn't wanna kill the pastor. I just wanted to take away his ability of getting another woman and doing this same stuff to another family. I missed the spot that I was aiming for though, and I shot him in his leg instead. The judge told me that if I would have shot the pastor one inch above the waist or if I would've squeezed the trigger two times, hitting him twice in the leg, my charge wouldn't have been Assault & Battery it would've been Attempted Murder. Meaning that I would have been spending the rest of my teenage life in a juvenile facility or even trialed as an adult and faced anywhere from seven to ninety-nine years in prison.

Author, Kevin Guillard, is from Baton Rouge, Louisiana. He gained a passion for writing while he was in the fourth grade; back when he used rhymes and lyrics as a tool for expressing himself. In high school it grew into poetry. There was a lot of other writing in between high school and the time Kevin turned 25 which is when he wrote his first novel entitled "Hood Struggle." Hood Struggle was published in October, 2013. In November, 2014 he opened a company called A.R. Publications, LLC (America's Rawest Publications, LLC) in which he plans to introduce the raw and uncut literature in the United States. He is currently working on his second novel.